Gunfire.

The sound Axel hoped to never hear again had him grabbing the woman and pushing her toward the truck. The men with the flashlights were shooting at them!

"Get down low," he warned. "Hurry." He ushered her inside the cab before jumping in beside her. Camo, who had ducked at the sound of the gunshots, immediately was alert by this new person.

"It's okay, Camo. She's a friend." He scooted the dog over and glanced at the woman he wasn't anywhere close to being convinced was a friend. Who knew what she'd gotten involved in that had intruded on his peaceful existence, but the soldier in him wouldn't let him leave her to those wolves.

He sped away under heavy fire. Several shots came far too close. Axel swerved around a curve and glanced in his rearview mirror thinking they'd escaped the armed men on foot. But multiple sets of headlights assured him that they had vehicles waiting near the road.

He'd question the woman later once they were safe. Staying alive was his only priority right now.

Mary Alford is a *USA TODAY* bestselling author who loves giving her readers the unexpected, combining unforgettable characters with unpredictable plots that result in stories the reader can't put down. Her titles have been finalists for several awards, including the Daphne du Maurier, the Beverly, the Maggie and the Selah. She and her husband live in the heart of Texas in the middle of seventy acres with two cats and one dog. Learn more about Mary at www.maryalford.net.

Books by Mary Alford

Love Inspired Suspense

Forgotten Past
Rocky Mountain Pursuit
Deadly Memories
Framed for Murder
Standoff at Midnight Mountain
Grave Peril
Amish Country Kidnapping
Amish Country Murder
Covert Amish Christmas
Shielding the Amish Witness
Dangerous Amish Showdown
Snowbound Amish Survival
Amish Wilderness Survival
Amish Country Ransom
Deadly Mountain Escape
Ambush in the Mountains

Visit the Author Profile page at LoveInspired.com.

Ambush in the Mountains

MARY ALFORD

If you purchased this book without a cover you should be aware that this book is stolen property. It was reported as "unsold and destroyed" to the publisher, and neither the author nor the publisher has received any payment for this "stripped book."

Ambush in the Mountains deals with topics that some readers may find difficult, including human trafficking.

LOVE INSPIRED® SUSPENSE
INSPIRATIONAL ROMANCE

Recycling programs for this product may not exist in your area.

ISBN-13: 978-1-335-98003-8

Ambush in the Mountains

For questions and comments about the quality of this book, please contact us at CustomerService@Harlequin.com.

Love Inspired
22 Adelaide St. West, 41st Floor
Toronto, Ontario M5H 4E3, Canada
www.LoveInspired.com

Printed in Lithuania

FSC www.fsc.org
MIX
Paper | Supporting responsible forestry
FSC® C021394

He healeth the broken in heart,
and bindeth up their wounds.
—*Psalm* 147:3

To those who are free and to those who are captive still. We pray. Continually and always. Until all are free from the bounds of human trafficking and those responsible are brought to justice.
Because no life is for sale!

ONE

Something soft and wet touched her face. It was so cold. Snow. Happy memories made her smile. Just for a second, she was back on the farm with her *mamm* and *daed*. Younger *bruders*, Peter and Eli. Winters were always such fun in her Amish community. After chores were finished, she'd take Peter and Eli to go ice skating on the pond near their farm. *Mamm* would make them hot chocolate.

But this wasn't Ohio, and those memories weren't real any longer. At times Summer wondered if they'd ever been. Maybe her brain had created happy memories in order to deal with the nightmare.

This was real. *He* was real. His angry face replaced the sweetness in her mind. With a gasp, Summer's eyes flew open. Darkness surrounded her. Waking so quickly left her disoriented. Her breath fogged the air in front of her. So cold. It had been snowing for a while—the white flakes covered her clothes and hair.

She hadn't meant to fall asleep. Just rest her aching body for a little while. The hours of tramping through the woods, stumbling and sometimes falling, had taken their toll. She'd only wanted to take a break for a second and had ended up wasting valuable time.

"No, no, no." Summer struggled to a sitting position, difficult with the added weight of the baby. Being eight months pregnant made it difficult to do most things.

How much time had passed? *Please let it be only a few minutes.* The sky above revealed nothing but pretty white flakes, yet her sweatshirt was covered in snow.

Summer shivered from the cold and listened over the panic beat of her heart. Were those voices or the noises of the woods?

It had barely been daylight when she'd slipped out of the house while Ray and the others slept. Many hours had past, and a storm had moved.

I'll find you and when I do, I'll kill you.

He'd warned what he'd do to her if she escaped. Ray had bragged about the ones who tried. He'd told her he'd buried them where no one would ever find them.

She had to go. Had to keep moving. With the help of the tree she'd rested beneath, Summer slowly rose, her swollen feet shooting pins and needles up her legs. The mere effort of standing exhausted her. How could she possibly go any farther?

The temptation to give up and accept her fate was great. After all, she deserved it.

"No!" She wouldn't feel sorry for herself. She'd escaped. Summer touched her burgeoning midsection. She'd saved her baby's life by running. Now was not the time to give up, because it wasn't just her—she had to think about the baby.

According to Ray, Summer had aged out long ago and was all used up. She wasn't the type of girl his clients would request anymore. They only wanted young women between the ages of thirteen and twenty. Instead of letting her go like he promised, he'd forced her to "handle the other girls' needs" as he'd put it. That meant keeping them calm and cooperating. Ray believed that if the other girls saw her still working for him at twenty-six, they'd think the same was possible for them eventually.

But that wasn't the case at all. Summer wasn't working for Ray because she had any other choice. It was out of sheer survival.

She'd memorized as many of the girls' names and faces as possible to help find them in the future. Ray had gotten so used to having her around that he'd become careless with keeping his secrets. She knew things and she'd managed to download a lot of Ray's files onto a thumb drive, including one folder labeled simply "Barn," which she hadn't been able to open.

She'd promised herself that when the opportunity came, she'd escape and tell the police everything. But that was before Ray told her he had cops on his payroll. Her world had collapsed that day. There was no one to turn to for help except herself.

When Ray found out he was going to be a father, he wanted to get rid of the baby…until he'd figured out he could get money for the child.

There was no way she'd let Ray sell her baby.

He'd thought he broke her will to escape long ago, but he had no idea what she'd do to save her baby.

Drawing in a handful of breaths, Summer started walking again as fast as the exhaustion in her limbs would allow. By now, he would know she'd run. He'd send men to look for her because he couldn't afford to let her live. She'd been part of their operation for a long time. She knew things. Terrible things.

Summer. The name he'd given her didn't fit, but she'd been Summer for so long she barely remembered the woman she was before. Elizabeth Wyse was an innocent eighteen-year-old Amish girl who met up with the wrong person while on *rumspringa*, and her life had changed forever. She'd lost her family and everything she held precious, and had been plunged into a seedy world of human trafficking for more than eight years.

Tears she hadn't allowed herself to release for so long scalded her cheeks, and she swiped them away with an angry hand.

Before escaping, Summer had hidden the thumb drive in one of the walls of the living room. It was at the house where Ray and the other members of the ring stayed along with the girls. It would be bad for her if Ray found out she'd copied his files.

More noises behind her confirmed that what she'd heard earlier wasn't simply sounds of the woods. She jerked in that direction. Someone was coming. She'd wasted too much time resting and now they were close. There was no time for self-pity. She imagined Ray's angry face and it spurred her on. If he caught her, he'd hurt her badly.

Gott, I need Your strength.

Her body felt lighter as she broke into a run. Up ahead the woods thinned out. Lights appeared. Different from a flashlight. They were much bigger. Car headlights. She'd reached a road. A vehicle was coming. *Please let it be help and not him.*

Stumbling, she kept her focus on the headlights. If she could reach the car before they found her…

She half slid, half tripped out onto the road, her breathing coming in ragged gasps. Summer turned toward the vehicle. It approached much faster than she imagined.

As she stared at the growing headlights, she wondered if the driver would see her in time. She held on to her baby as the truck continued to barrel down on her.

Her legs gave out and she dropped to her knees, unable to

find the strength to stay standing. Would she and her child die here? For years, she'd prayed for death, but now she wanted to live. Wanted to be the mother her baby deserved. She didn't want Ray to write her ending.

Axel Sterling stomped on the brake pedal and jerked the steering wheel hard to the left—away from the woman in the middle of the road. The headlights captured her frightened expression. Why wasn't she moving?

"Don't let me hit her." The woman's swollen belly had him begging God for help. He'd killed enough in his lifetime. Most had been enemy soldiers. She wasn't.

"Hang on, Camo." The Belgian Malinois that had been his constant companion was tossed against the door as the car skidded across the pavement. The dog whimpered. "Sorry, buddy." Axel grabbed for him and scooted him closer. He'd do his best to protect his friend.

The brakes caught and locked. He could smell burning rubber. Axel let the dog go and grabbed the wheel with both hands, worried the truck would flip.

"Come on!" he yelled and fought to keep from barreling off the side of the mountain and to certain death. He white-knuckled the steering wheel for several more yards before it came to a shuddering stop.

Axel blew out a big shaky breath and held up his trembling hands. He looked over his shoulder. The woman had managed to stand. She'd turned toward his vehicle.

What was she doing out here in the first place with one of the worst storms of the season moving in? He had no business being out here himself. Axel's only excuse was, he'd thought he had time to reach the store, grab his needed supplies and get home before the brunt of it hit, which wasn't supposed to be until dark. He'd been wrong. The storm had turned the late afternoon to night before he made it home and the skies had dumped snow at an alarming rate.

Axel opened the cab door. Camo's full attention was on the woman. He barked aggressively, as if realizing there was more to the situation than simply saving a frightened young woman.

Camo had been a scout and patrol dog for the military until he retired and Axel had taken him in. The canine soldier had experienced a lot of danger in his lifetime. The hackles raised on his back confirmed that whatever was happening here was going to be bad.

The woman's frightened eyes went to the dog. She seemed to shrink away from the threat she perceived Camo represented.

"Stay," Axel told the dog and because he'd seen combat himself and knew sometimes the most innocent of things were not, he tucked his handgun beneath his coat and hurried over to help the woman who was noticeably pregnant.

"Are you hurt?" he asked when he reached her side. She instinctively put space between them. The reaction made him wonder if it was because of Camo's barking or him? What was she doing out here alone in weather such as this? She wore only a sweatshirt and jeans and no coat despite the cold. Her feet were clad in flip-flops. Not exactly appropriate attire for this weather. Was she running from someone who had hurt her?

Axel slipped out of his heavy down jacket and started to place it around her shoulders, but she backed farther away, her dark eyes filled with terror.

"I'm not going to hurt you," he said gently. "I want to help. Are you lost?" She certainly didn't appear to be a hiker in those clothes. Her blond hair was soaked from the falling snow. Her cheeks sunken. Eyes hollow and filled with a dread that went much deeper than being lost in the woods.

He took a step back. "My name is Axel."

Past her shoulder, he spotted four flashlights weaving through the woods.

She jerked around. "Oh, no. Please, you can't let him take me."

Axel tugged the coat tighter around her. "Then come with me." She hesitated only a second before following him to the truck, still keeping her distance.

Two feet from the back, a sound he hoped to never hear again had him grabbing the woman and pushing her toward the cover of the truck. Gunfire. The people with the flashlights were shooting at them!

"Get down low," Axel warned and steadied her when she stumbled. He whipped his handgun out and returned fire, forcing the shooters to take cover.

"Hurry." Axel grabbed her arm, ignoring the way she tried to pull free. He ushered her inside the cab before jumping in beside her. Camo, who had ducked at the sound of the gunshots, growled low immediately on alert by this new person.

"It's okay, Camo. She's a friend." He scooted the dog over and glanced at the woman who he wasn't anywhere close to being convinced was a friend. Who knew what she'd gotten herself involved in that had intruded in his peaceful existence? Yet the soldier in him wouldn't let him leave her to those wolves.

He fired the truck engine up and shoved it into Drive before speeding away. Several shots came far too close. Axel swerved around a curve and was grateful that the roads weren't slick enough to send them flying down the side of the mountain. He glanced in his rearview mirror, thinking they'd escaped the shooters on foot. But multiple sets of headlights assured him they had vehicles waiting near the road.

Staying alive was his only priority right now. He'd question the woman later once they were safe.

"Put your seat belt on." The words came out a little too sharply. "There's a small road up ahead. If I can make it without being spotted, we stand a chance at losing them."

He glanced at Camo. The dog watched the stranger with open distrust. "Camo, get on the floorboard."

The canine grumbled but hopped down at her feet while keeping a close eye on her.

Once she'd secured the seat belt, Axel killed the lights including the interior ones. She screamed as the world around them went pitch-black.

"It's okay," he said. "I don't want them to see where we're going." He needed to put space between them and those headlights so their attackers couldn't pick up the change in direction.

He rounded another curve in the road and squinted through the windshield at nothing but darkness. "The road is on the right-hand side and it's hard to see."

She leaned against the door as if to put as much distance between them as possible.

Axel realized he didn't know what to call her and asked her name. When she didn't respond, he looked her way again. She wasn't giving away any answers, and her huge brown eyes were glued to him as if she expected him to attack her at any minute.

It was going to be difficult to get her to open up to him when she didn't trust him. He let the questions go for now. "Can you help me watch for the road? It should be coming up soon."

Another look confirmed she still clung to the door, but she leaned forward, searching the darkness past the windshield. Strands of her wet hair fell across her face. She tucked it behind her ear. It was then that he noticed a scar across her hand. Someone had hurt her. The men coming after her? What was going on?

"There." She pointed to what could barely be considered an opening.

"I see it." Axel slowed enough to make the turn. The truck slid sideways, and the woman screamed again.

Camo looked up at him without concern. They knew each other and trust had been well established.

Once he had the vehicle straightened and under control, Axel watched the rearview mirror. "So far, I don't see anyone." He slowed enough to traverse the pitted road without causing damage to the truck. After they'd traveled a while he said, "We should be safe enough to use the lights again." Axel flipped them on and the countryside around them illuminated.

His mind mentally calculated what route he'd have to take to reach his place. This road intersected with one of the main county roads. If he took it, he could eventually backtrack to his home.

While Axel tried to untangle what he could possibly be dealing with that would bring armed men after this woman, a far more disturbing thought had him wondering if they had the ability to track the vehicle through his license plate. If so, his mountain sanctuary would be compromised.

Axel wasn't one to do anything without a plan. To formulate one, he needed answers from her now.

"Who are those men back there?" He waited for her to speak but she just stared at him with those huge dark eyes.

"Look, I'm trying to help you, but I don't understand what's happening."

If possible, she shrank even farther away from him.

"At least tell me your name," he said, unable to keep his frustration out of his tone.

Camo, as if sensing her distress, seemed to accept her into his space. He licked her hand. The gesture had her staring at the dog for the longest time before a smile spread across her face.

Nice going, boy.

Camo might have been a soldier in his previous career, but he'd adjusted okay to civilian life, and he enjoyed attention on his terms. The dog had a way of sensing when Axel's darkness came upon him, and he'd usually do something as simple as lie down at his feet or lick his hand like he had hers.

"My name is Summer." Tears glistened in her eyes as she spoke in a shaky voice.

A small victory in Axel's opinion. "Nice to meet you, Summer. You're safe now."

She scrubbed her hands across her face. "I'm not. He's coming after me."

"Who are you talking about?"

She set her chin and refused to answer.

Axel tried another tactic. "I only want to help." That she didn't believe him was clear. "Where are you from? I can help you get back home." He wondered if he could reach out to her family to let them know she was safe before going to the sheriff to report the crime.

She shook her head. "No. That's not possible."

"Why not?" He looked her way when she didn't respond.

"Because… I—I can't go back there. Not like this." She touched her swollen belly.

Axel sensed she wasn't going to tell him anything more about her past.

"How far along are you?"

Summer hesitated for the longest time. She didn't trust him. He believed there were few people she did trust.

"Eight months, I think," she said in barely a whisper. "When he found out I was pregnant, at first he wanted to get rid of the child, but then he figured out a way to sell the baby. I couldn't let that happen."

Disgust rose in Axel's throat. His hands tightened on the wheel. "Who is this man?"

She wiped at her face once more. "I don't know."

Was it true or was she somehow protecting this monster?

Axel let go of his misgivings. "We'll figure it out. Right now, we need to put as much space as possible between us and those shooters."

She turned away and stared out the side window. Her story was going to be horrendous when it came but she wasn't ready to share it yet.

Axel's attention returned to the bumpy road ahead. He of all people understood how hard it was to return to the life you left behind. He'd been struggling to find his place since he'd returned from the war. He'd gone home and wanted to fit back into his old life in Colorado but nothing about it felt right anymore. And so, he'd traveled around the country looking for someplace to feel like he belonged. Then Brayden told him about Elk Ridge, Montana. When he'd ended up in almost total isolation on a cabin atop a mountain in the Tobacco Root Mountains, Axel realized this was where he felt the most normal. He'd bought the place right away.

The army had given him a purpose. He'd excelled at becoming a sniper. Life was going well. He'd realized he'd found someone to love for the first time in his life…

Axel shut down that way of thinking before the darkness could set in. Summer needed his help. He had a purpose. A mission. That he understood.

The blackness in his rearview mirror made him grateful. At least for the moment, those dangerous men hadn't caught the diversion.

Camo settled on the floorboards with a harumph and closed his eyes, content with the peace of the moment. In war, a soldier learned to take advantage of the downtimes because you never knew when they would disappear.

The woman seated beside Axel was far from being at peace. Her eyes were glued to the side mirror with good reason. Those men wouldn't be coming after her with such force if she didn't pose a threat.

A pit formed in his stomach. It warned him this was far from over. They weren't going to simply let her get away and give up.

"Are you hungry?" he asked and remembered he'd purchased some snacks for the ride home. "There's some chips and bottled water in the bag there. Oh, and a couple of candy bars." His guilty pleasure was the occasional binge on junk food. "I realize it's probably not the healthiest of snacks," he said when she hesitated. "Especially for the baby." But it was all he had.

She opened the grocery bag and dug out the chips. "I'm starving." She tore the bag open and munched several chips before holding the bag out to Axel.

"No thanks. You enjoy." He'd make a more nutritious meal once they reached the house.

Now that his pulse had finally returned to normal, he began working out the details of getting to his cabin without taking any of the main county roads. Unfortunately, he couldn't avoid the one coming up.

Once they reached the cabin, he'd call the sheriff on his satellite phone. Everything would be okay. So, why didn't it feel that way? Why couldn't he relax?

Because of the fear written all over her face, and the truth he knew in his gut.

TWO

She wiped her cheese-dust-covered fingers on her jeans. With the gnawing hunger abated, Summer drank deeply from a water bottle.

When she'd managed to escape while Ray and the rest of his people were sleeping, Summer had one thought and that was saving her child.

Ray had given her more freedom since she'd begun working for the ring. She wasn't locked away at night like the other girls. Ray believed she'd do whatever he told her to…even give up her baby.

Unfamiliar tears stung her eyes once more. They sickened her because they represented weakness. The things she'd been forced to do had made her numb on the inside. Yet as much as she tried to admonish the tears away, they wouldn't stop coming. It seemed as if all those pent-up emotions had been set free and she couldn't will them away.

"Are you okay?" The man who said his name was Axel asked as if he really did care. There was concern in his blue eyes.

"I'm fine," she said in a tone that sounded harsh. She owed him hers and her baby's lives, but that didn't mean she trusted him. Summer had learned men hurt you. "I—I'm sorry I haven't thanked you for saving me."

"It's okay and you're welcome. I'm glad I came along when I did. Where were you coming from?" He waited for an answer she wouldn't give before asking again, "Who are those men, Summer?"

She flinched at the sincerity on Axel's face. Ray had pretended to care about her and had her believing he loved her. He'd convinced her to leave her home and everyone she trusted and then he'd hurt her badly. Forced her to do things she didn't understand and had seemed unimaginable. The love he'd confessed evaporated, and the real monster remained in all his cruelty.

She was just one of many young women Ray had misled into trusting him. Like her, the other girls had been every bit as convinced he meant those words of love until he'd gotten them away from their families and anyone who could help them.

"Your family must be worried about you." Axel glanced over. "If you tell me where they live, I can help get you home." She almost believed him. Summer stared down at the dog, who had opened his eyes at their brief exchange. Camo seemed to realize she needed a friend and licked her hand again while she petted his head.

Eight years. Had it really been more than eight years since she'd turned eighteen and made that fateful mistake to talk to Ray even though every instinct in her body warned her not to.

But it was at the end of her *rumspringa*, and she wanted to try new things. Be daring.

"My place is on the other side of the mountain. You can warm up while I call the sheriff. He can reach out to your parents and let them know you're safe."

"No—you can't. No police." Ray's bragging came to mind. He'd told her that he had people in places to protect his operation, and then he'd looked at her and she believed he'd meant he had people in law enforcement working for him.

"Why not?" he said gently and touched her arm. Summer immediately jerked free and put as much space as she could between them. She hated this reaction, but after the things she'd been forced to endure because of Ray, she'd developed an aversion to being touched.

"Sorry." Axel quickly removed his hand, those sharp blue eyes held hers, waiting for an explanation she had no plan to give.

Axel apparently gave up on getting answers and focused on the road while Summer returned to that dark place once more. In the beginning, Summer believed Ray loved her. She couldn't imagine her luck at finding someone as nice to love her back. When he'd suggested leaving the Amish way of life for good, it had seemed impossible to consider, but the more time she spent with him, the more she wanted a life with Ray no matter what it cost her. She'd find a way to stay in touch with her family.

Summer had snuck out late one night after her parents and *bruders* had fallen asleep and met Ray on the road near their house.

She'd giggled when he swept her into his arms. Summer never imagined being so happy. And then…

Everything changed. He'd taken her to a run-down farmhouse and told her what was expected of her. When she'd cried, he made her believe everything was her fault. He'd demoralized her to the point of thinking her parents wouldn't want her back. He was all she had.

Summer clenched her hands into fists until her jagged nails dug into her palms. Keeping a clear head was all that had helped her escape Ray.

As the time grew closer to when she'd deliver the baby,

Summer knew she had to make her move. She'd been so terrified. When she'd reached the front hall without being spotted, Summer had swung the door open. The creaking sound it made almost had her giving up. But then she thought about her baby, and she'd run.

She'd snatched a steak knife from the kitchen the day before because it was all she could find to use as a weapon. Having it made her feel somewhat protected.

"Camo likes you."

She didn't need to look at Axel to realize he was watching her, probably trying to draw her out of her shell.

"And Camo doesn't like just anyone," Axel was saying.

As if to bring the point home, Camo laid his head in Summer's lap. She couldn't not smile. The dog reminded her of her family dog, Pepper. She'd loved that dog. Was he still alive after so long?

Tears struggled to be set free and she bit down hard on her bottom lip until she tasted blood. A coping mechanism she'd used to get through all those horrific experiences. If she ever truly let go of her guard, she'd be crying for days.

Summer patted the dog's head and felt inside her jeans pocket where the cold metal of the knife gave her some sense of being in control.

Axel slowed the truck to a stop, forcing her attention to him.

"What are you doing?" She searched his face, waiting for him to reveal his true self.

"There's an intersection coming up. I'm worried."

She understood. Ray and his evil people weren't likely to give up so easily. "What should we do?" She forced the words out.

Summer so wanted to trust this man who had rescued

her, but after everything she'd gone through, it was hard to make that leap.

He looked behind them. "We can't take the chance of returning the way we came. Eventually, those men will circle back. If they have any knowledge of the countryside, they'll know about the upcoming intersection. Wait here. I'll take a look." He got out and started walking down the road in front of them, the headlights picking up his sure steps. Snow covered his dark blond hair and plaid shirt. Summer glanced down and realized she still wore his jacket. It must be freezing out and yet he hadn't asked for the garment back. A simple act of kindness like this surely was genuine.

When he rounded the bend in the road and disappeared from sight, fear pressed in on all sides. Summer stroked the dog's fur with one hand and held on to the knife with the other. She counted the seconds, another way of coping when a situation became too much for her to get through on her own. She'd count.

One minute passed. She kept counting. At five minutes he reappeared, and she breathed out a relieved sigh. Camo barked his happiness when Axel got back in.

"I don't see anything. The road that intersects is one of the main county roads. Thankfully, we don't have to be on it too long."

He looked at her—waiting for a response she couldn't give—before he put the truck in gear and started slowly down the road. As he neared the intersection, Axel shut off the lights once more. The darkness was terrifying.

"So far so good," Axel said almost to himself. He rolled to a stop at the sign and looked both ways before turning left.

Summer watched the side mirror. It couldn't be this easy. She knew better. Ray had taken great pleasure in telling her about what he'd done to the girls who thought they could escape him, and it had been brutal.

If he found her, Ray would make her pay for leaving and he'd kill Axel for helping her.

Axel braked hard. Summer grabbed the door handle to keep from being thrown forward despite the seat belt.

"What is it?" She looked his way, but Axel was staring straight ahead. Her attention flew to the windshield and the darkness beyond. Lights glowed almost as if suspended in midair. A heartbeat later, Summer realized it was interior car lights. Soon, the rest of the vehicle became clear as her eyes adjusted. The driver had pulled the car sideways onto the road to block any oncoming traffic.

"It's him. It's Ray." The words flew out before she could stop them.

"Hold on." Axel shoved the truck into Reverse and flew backward until they'd reached the turnoff road. Once he was even with it, he hit Drive and sped down the road.

Summer looked behind them. "They're coming after us." More than one set of lights now followed.

Axel handled the vehicle skillfully. "We've got to get off the road. I noticed a place a little farther up."

She wasn't sure what he meant but she didn't see a viable way to leave the road that didn't sound frightening.

"From what I could tell, the vehicles behind us are all cars," Axel said. "They won't be able to make it through the rough terrain. At best, it will take a four-wheel-drive vehicle like this."

At best.

He slowed enough to put the truck in four-wheel drive before edging into the woods on Summer's side.

"Help me watch for obstacles," he told her. "We can't afford to use the lights and have them pick up our location."

Tree branches slapped the sides of the truck as Axel did his best to maneuver through them.

Summer leaned forward trying to see in near impossible conditions. “Wait, there’s a large tree coming up on my side.”

Axel squinted through the windshield. “I see it.” He inched the truck past it while barely keeping from clipping another on his side.

Camo whined as the vehicle rocked back and forth and climbed precariously over downed limbs and tree stumps. The dog jumped up onto the seat and fixed his attention on Axel.

“It’s okay, buddy.” Axel patted his friend’s head.

But was it?

Summer spotted lights in the side mirror and jerked around. “They’ve reached the place where we went off-road.”

Axel glanced quickly at the rearview mirror. “They’re trying to follow.” The move clearly caught him by surprise. “They won’t make it far, but still…”

The lead car’s headlights entered the woods.

Summer covered her stomach with her hands. Her baby. She hadn’t realized what it was like to love someone she didn’t know until she’d felt the baby kick. That was when Summer had known—she wasn’t going to let Ray sell her baby. She couldn’t let him capture her again. She’d fight with everything she had to keep that from happening.

“We need help, Summer, but unfortunately my sat phone is at my place.” Axel explained that a sat phone connected the phone to networks by radio link through satellites orbiting the Earth instead of cell towers. Apparently it proved to be more reliable. “Without it, we have no way to call anyone.” He looked her way. “In other words, we’re on our own.”

A shiver chased down her back. If they reached his cabin

safely, he'd want to call and report the attack. She couldn't let that happen. Couldn't risk Ray's mole within the police force alerting him to where she was.

The lead car's headlights caught up with the back of the truck.

"They're gaining!" Summer couldn't control the panic in her voice.

"Hold on to something." Axel punched the gas. With one hand she grabbed the door and with the other she tugged Camo closer.

Behind them, a rapid succession of loud pops had her turning.

"Gunshots." Axel eyed her. "They're shooting at us again. Get down."

Summer did her best to get out of sight, but it was hard with the baby.

The bullets reached them and bounced off the truck bed.

"How are they getting past all that debris?" Axel said in amazement.

One bullet hit the back window and it shattered on contact. Cold air and snow whipped in. Axel automatically ducked then rose enough to see over the dash.

"What's happening?" Summer yelled over the noise of gunfire.

"There's more than one car in the woods now." From his low stance, Axel glanced behind them as the truck climbed over downed trees and kept moving at a steady pace.

A sharp pain shot through Summer's midsection, and she let the dog go to grab hold of her baby, closing her eyes.

Axel saw her expression. "Are you okay?"

"It's just a cramp. I need to sit up." She did and prayed the pain would pass. After a few deep breaths it abated. "I'm okay."

Axel blew out a breath and nodded. Another round of shots had her jumping.

"They're too far to reach us now," he said. "It looks as if the lead car is stuck. We have the advantage. Let's keep going."

Summer kept her attention behind them for the longest time. Had they really escaped?

Axel's hands relaxed a little on the steering wheel. "I haven't seen an attack like this since I left Afghanistan."

He was a soldier. That explained the way he'd protected her. Summer shifted a little to study his profile. His strong jaw was covered in slightly darker stubble. A small bump on the bridge of his nose had her wondering if it were natural or if his nose had been broken at one time. He wore such a serious look on his face.

Axel turned in time to see her watching. "Are you feeling better?"

Summer nodded and faced forward. The darkness beyond the windshield was filled with unknowns just like her life. "Where does this lead?" she asked in an unsteady voice.

Axel cranked the wheel hard to miss a fallen tree that had come up almost too quick to dodge. "That was close. I'm going to have to turn on the headlights. The woods are getting thicker."

He flipped them on and the world in front of them came out of the darkness. Summer got her first real look at what Axel had been fighting. The floor of the woods was littered with trees in various stages of decay.

"There's a small road coming up once we top this ridge and head down the other side." He pointed to the incline they were heading for. "It will connect to another that leads to my place up on the top of the mountain."

A shiver of fear returned along with her distrust. Axel

had saved her life and he seemed to be genuinely trying to help her, but Ray had appeared believable as well. She'd thought he'd cared about her until the real Ray showed up and the truth became clear. He'd kidnapped her and forced her into prostitution.

"Is one of those men the father?" Axel asked quietly. "Is that why they're coming after you with so much manpower?"

Saying the words aloud made what she'd become real. How could she tell him the things she'd been forced to do to survive? The men who hadn't bothered to wonder how old she or the other girls were. Or if they were being treated badly. After she'd aged out, Ray had kept her for himself. She'd hated those times. He had asked to hear stories about growing up Amish in Ohio and then he'd make fun of her simple ways.

She'd thought when she became pregnant, things would be different. Ray might actually look forward to having the baby, but nothing could be further from the truth.

She hung her head without answering.

Axel's deep blue eyes bored into hers. "What's really going on, Summer."

If she told, he'd look at her the way the other men had, as if she were worthless. Once more tears of frustration blurred everything in sight. Would there ever be a time when she didn't feel like nothing?

"Hey, it's okay," he said gently. "No matter what you've gone through, everything is going to be okay. I'm not going to let any of those men hurt you again."

Wouldn't it be nice to believe him? Summer scrubbed her hand over her eyes and glanced at Camo, who appeared to be watching her. The dog laid his head in her lap again and she lost a little of her heart to him. She choked out a laugh, the sound of it foreign. She hadn't laughed in a long time.

It gave her hope. Maybe it was possible to survive Ray and find her place in the world again.

Though she didn't say it, Axel believed Summer had escaped from a human trafficking ring. He couldn't imagine the things she'd endured, probably from a young age. She couldn't be more than in her mid-twenties.

Every time he made a move, she shrank away, putting as much distance between them as the truck's cab would allow. He'd tried to assure her she could trust him and finally resorted to showing her.

At least one car was disabled. He'd counted three sets of headlights before. Axel tried to remember how many had chased them after he'd saved Summer.

"It looks as if it's stuck." Summer had seen the same thing he had.

Axel grunted an answer. He didn't want to tell her as much, but he was worried. She'd mentioned one name. Ray. If he was calling the shots like Summer's reactions seemed to confirm, then for whatever reason, they weren't going to give up so easily. Those men had come after her with guns blazing. Summer was important enough for them to kill to get her back. Axel had his handgun and the shotgun he carried with him but that was it.

"Can you shoot?" he asked, the question clearly surprising her.

"I've never fired a weapon, but I can learn."

Would he be making a mistake arming a frightened amateur who clearly didn't trust him? He'd hate for her to turn the weapon on him out of some misguided attempt to protect herself because of what'd she'd survived.

"Why do you ask?" she pressed when Axel's thoughts ran a mile a minute.

He decided they both needed to trust each other and that meant him telling her what he suspected would happen when they reached the road.

"I'm afraid there may be men waiting for us." He watched the horrified expression that had only just begun to evaporate return in full force.

"There must be another way out. I can't go back with him."

"There isn't," he told her. The alarm on her face was clearly justified. Behind them, several men had flashlights and were coming after them on foot. He had to act fast. Sitting still would allow the pursuers time to catch up.

Axel killed the lights and jerked the wheel to the right. "We can't use the lights if we stand a chance at escaping. I'm not sure if this is the best way to go since it will basically take us back to the road where they were waiting for us before."

Summer looked behind them. "Do you think they'll figure out which way we're going?"

He'd made a promise to himself to tell her the truth no matter how bad. "Eventually. I'm just hoping not before we have the chance to get away."

Summer returned to petting Camo as if it gave her comfort. Camo didn't mind. He'd developed a softness for her. Axel was glad for the distraction his pooch provided. He needed time to think of what to do.

What was happening went way beyond anything Axel felt equipped to deal with despite his training. He'd been living in almost total isolation in his mountaintop haven trying to heal.

He'd lost so much to the war. With only two months before being discharged, Axel realized he'd fallen in love with his childhood friend and fellow soldier. He'd planned to tell

Erin about his feelings when her unit was attacked and she was killed. He never got to tell her how he felt about her. Instead, he was left with a broken heart that wouldn't heal. He'd become the shell of the person he was today, seeking out his own company because he wasn't fit to be with anyone else. Except Camo.

Axel's only neighbors were the Amish couple who lived down below him. They ran a rescue mission for animals as well as a farm. Abram took in all sorts of animals including retired dogs of service. That's where Axel had met Camo. They'd clicked from the start. Both had seen things in battle they wished they could forget.

Axel carefully weaved his way along through the massive amount of trees that were dead due to beetles. He kept his attention on what little he could see beyond the hood and tried to stay ahead of wrecking the truck. They couldn't afford to lose their only means of transportation. The snow was the first of the fall, but it was dark, and the temperatures were below freezing.

Not to mention armed men were hunting them down.

He hit the brakes, startling Summer and Camo. He'd barely missed a massive tree trunk by inches. Axel pulled in a shaky breath and let it go. "Sorry. That was close." He backed up. "I can't see a way around it from here. Sit tight. I'll have a look." The men with the flashlights were still some distance.

"No, wait." The fear in her voice stopped him.

"It's okay," he said gently. "I'll be right back. I'm just going to see if I can find a way past the tree." He waited for a long moment. She'd been through unimaginable things. A little patience was necessary.

"Okay," she said softly.

"You're safe, I promise." With that assurance, he got

out and carefully closed the door so as to not alert anyone below.

Bitter cold nailed him the second he left the protection of the truck. This storm had hit quickly. According to all weather reports, it would arrive late in the evening. He'd managed to grab the necessary groceries for himself and Camo, plus feed for the two mares and handful of cows at his place. Axel had been a couple miles outside the nearest town, Elk Ridge, when the gray foreboding clouds had let loose, and snow mixed with ice had Axel worried if he'd make it home without incident. He'd thought the weather would be his only problem.

The downed spruce was much bigger than he could move by himself. He had a winch on the back of the truck, but the time it would take to move the limb, not to mention the sound, proved too risky.

He walked a little way to the right, searching for a better spot to take the truck through. The choices weren't great, but Axel found one place that might work.

He returned to the truck. The fear on Summer's face hadn't eased any.

"Can you move it?" she asked.

He shook his head. "No, but I found another way around."

He put the truck in Reverse and backed up. "It's going to be tight."

The brake and backup lights were probably giving away their location. A quick look behind confirmed the men had discovered their change of direction. "They know where we are." He shoved the truck into Drive and headed toward a narrow opening between trees. Sparks flew from both sides as the tree trunks scraped across the vehicle.

Camo barked aggressively at the noise. As soon as the

truck cleared, Axel pushed it as fast as he dared while once more Summer clutched the door.

"The road shouldn't be much farther, but I'm worried," he admitted. "They know the direction we're going by now. There might be cars there to cut us off."

He kept the speed up until the road came into view. No matter what he found waiting for them, he couldn't slow down. Because Axel was convinced the terror he'd seen in Summer was real and he didn't want to find out what those men would do if they caught her again.

THREE

"There's a fence!" Summer screamed. "We can't make it through."

"We don't have a choice. We're going through it."

Summer grasped Camo and couldn't look at the barbed wire fence coming up too quickly. She kept her attention on Axel. He didn't appear afraid. Why didn't he appear afraid?

The front of the truck struck the gate hard. The resistance it gave to the speeding vehicle was only temporary but enough to throw Summer forward and then back when each strand of the wire snapped free.

Axel's attention was on the stretch of ditch that would prove as difficult as anything they'd survived so far.

"No. Axel!" she shrieked when the truck hit the ditch and vaulted into midair. Before Axel had time to warn her to hold on, it slammed onto the road hard. A loud pop had her attention jerking behind them expecting another shootout but there was nothing.

Summer closed her eyes and prayed hard.

Help us. Please, help us.

Axel brought the truck to a shuddering stop. "I think we may have blown a tire. Let me check." She wanted to warn him it was too dangerous. What if Ray had men waiting in the woods? What if those who had been following them caught up?

"We're safe for now," he said, reading her thoughts. "I don't see any sign of them. I'll only be a second." He hopped out and checked. It didn't take long before he returned and put the truck in Drive. "The front right tire is blown. But we'll have to keep going."

"Won't it destroy the wheel?"

"Probably." He tossed the word her way before putting the truck in gear. It sounded as if it were riding on a wooden block as Axel wrangled the injured wheel down the road.

Summer couldn't believe the things that had happened in just a short amount of time. Ray was determined to find her. He knew the things she'd seen. Enough to put him and his crew away for a long time. She had no doubt of the outcome if it came to keeping her alive to get the money for the baby or silencing her before she could reveal what she knew.

"Uh-oh."

Axel's words had her wrenching his way. His focus was behind them.

A set of headlights appeared. An innocent traveler or…?

"I can't afford to drive too fast on this bad tire." He ran a hand through his hair. "I think there's a smaller road coming up on the right. Unfortunately, it's going to take us farther away from my place." He kept his attention on the lights. "I just hope we make it before they catch us."

Thunk, thunk, thunk. Every turn of the blown wheel thumped along her stretched-thin nerves. She stared out the side window to keep track of the lights. They'd never make it. The vehicle was closing in on them at a rapid rate.

Soon, inches off their bumper, the driver struck the truck hard, sending them all forward in their seats.

Summer couldn't hold back the scream.

Another ram had Axel fighting for control as the truck careened toward the ditch.

"They're trying to run us off the road. I'm going to try something."

Summer anticipated his warning to hold on and grabbed for the door again.

He sped up enough to put space between them before he jerked the wheel hard to the left and the truck swung sideways then faced the approaching car. Axel turned the lights on bright.

When it became apparent what he had planned, Summer prayed all the harder.

Axel slammed the heavier truck into the oncoming car. The impact sent them spinning on the slick road. Axel hit the brakes and managed to stop despite the disabled tire.

The car driver's panicked expression flashed before them before he slammed into the ditch hard, lodging the vehicle nose first.

"They're getting out." Four men climbed from the vehicle and opened fire. Summer automatically ducked low as the bullets bounced off the cab and Axel spun his truck around and drove away as fast as possible.

"At least we won't have to worry about them coming after us on wheels." He gave her a lopsided grin before telling her it was safe to sit up.

Summer rose and noticed the men were standing in the middle of the road. One appeared to be talking on a phone. "Axel, they're calling for help."

His attention shifted from the space in front of them to the men.

Once more, he shut off the lights. "We need to get out of sight fast." He drove for some distance before they reached a small opening on the right side of the road. "There's our turn. I don't think they'll notice."

The blown tire clearly made it difficult to steer the vehicle.

"We should be out of sight enough to use the headlights again." He flipped them on. As soon as Summer glimpsed the road in front of them, her unease returned. It was barely big enough for the truck to fit down and it didn't appear to have been used in a long time. The recently fallen snow covered the road undisturbed.

All the trust she'd built for Axel evaporated as memories of that night returned. Ray had taken her down a road like this one leading to that farmhouse and the beginning of her eight-year-long nightmare.

"Are you sure this is the way?" she asked uneasily.

Axel checked they weren't being followed before answering. "This is the road. I realize it doesn't look like much, but my Amish friends use it often. They took me down it once. Very few people know about it. Even if the men behind us are familiar with the area, they may not know about this road. As you can see, if you weren't looking for it specifically, you would never know it was there." His gaze softened as he held hers.

He had friends who were Amish. Summer clenched her hands to keep from showing any reaction. She'd lived eighteen years in the Plain world of Ohio in the Holmes Community.

Until her *rumspringa*, Summer hadn't known there was life beyond her family and the community. When she and Hannah, her friend, had gone through their "running around time," they started hanging out at some of the *Englischer* businesses around town.

She still remembered the first time she'd seen Ray. He'd

looked so handsome and trustworthy. Ray had spotted them and come over. He'd flirted with her and Hannah before singling her out.

Summer told herself it was because he found her attractive. Now she knew the truth. Of the two of them, she was the most gullible.

"I don't know what you've gone through, Summer, but you can trust me. I would never hurt you." Axel's sincere voice broke through the memories of that time.

Trusting Axel still didn't sit well with her, but it was her only option right now. He pulled the wheel hard to the left to avoid a pit in the road. "We'll have to circle back to my place. Unfortunately, there aren't any houses around with phones. There's an Amish settlement nearby but they don't allow phones." He said it as if she didn't know. The words fell like knives to her heart. What she wouldn't give to be back at her family home helping her *mamm* with the evening meal. Doing chores along with *Daed* and her little brothers, Peter and Eli.

Through the years, she wondered if they thought about her. Summer hadn't told anyone she was running away with an *Englischer*. She'd simply run away in the middle of the night. Did her family try to find her through the years? Did they miss her as much as she missed them?

"Here's our road," Axel was saying. Summer pushed those memories aside. She wasn't that girl anymore.

"How are you holding up?" Axel asked with another captivating smile. "The road was rougher than I remembered."

"I'm…fine." She'd almost said *oke*. Just for a second, the past had bled into her reality. The language of her youth still came easy enough. Ray made her speak it so he could laugh at her and call her simple.

"You live amongst the Amish?" she asked because she

needed something to take her mind off everything she'd given up.

"I've lived near the small Amish settlement since..." He stopped. She wondered what secrets he had hidden. "My place is the last house up the mountain and some distance from the settlement, but there's one Amish couple who live close by." He looked her way briefly. "That's where I found Camo. He served in the military like me."

The dog watched him with wisdom that seemed to hint he understood exactly what Axel said.

She never realized dogs could be part of the military and told Axel as much.

"Oh, yes." Axel nodded. "They're used in all sorts of capacities from search and rescue, scout and patrol, guard and sentry as well as narcotics and weapons detection." He glanced down at the dog. "Camo, here, was a scout and patrol dog. According to Abram and Lainey, he was trained to work in silence in order to detect possible ambushes, snipers or other types of enemy attacks."

Summer was surprised. "What an amazing creature you are, Camo."

Axel smiled at her description, and she wished this moment of quiet reprieve could last forever. "According to what I've read about the scouts," he said, "they're a bit of an elite group among the military working dogs. Only dogs with both superior intelligence and a quiet disposition can be selected for this specialty. Scout and patrol dogs are generally sent out with their handlers to walk point during combat patrols, well ahead of the infantry patrol." He stopped. "Sorry, I'm probably boring you with so many details. Needless to say, I'm proud of Camo's service."

"Not at all." Summer was impressed. Though she loved their family dog, she wished she'd had one like Camo. Perhaps he would have helped her see the truth about Ray before she'd made the worst mistake of her life.

The familiar road to his cabin rose beneath the injured truck. It could barely be called a road actually. More like a path filled with gravel. He wondered how well the four-wheel-drive feature would work with the tire gone and on its rim. Under normal conditions, Axel was happy his place was two miles up the mountain and virtually inaccessible during the winter months except with his Jeep, which had snow chains on it.

"You live up here by yourself?" she asked.

Her distrust had returned, and he couldn't blame her. She didn't really know him, and they'd been thrown together in a difficult situation. He wanted to ask her the questions racing through his head but first he'd have to gain her trust. He just hoped there'd be time before the next attack because Axel had no doubt they hadn't seen the last of the assailants, and he needed to understand what they were up against.

His arms ached from forcing the truck to do as he wished. Once he got home, he'd get the tire changed and hope there wouldn't be any lasting damage to the vehicle.

As they drew closer to the top of the mountain, the path narrowed. On Summer's side there was a sheer drop-off that would mean certain death if one false move sent them over the side.

She grew increasingly uneasy watching the treacherous slope. Axel edged away from it for both their benefits.

"How do you get around in the winter?" she asked.

He told her about his Jeep. "It works well for traversing the snow."

The snow continued to fall heavier at this higher altitude, peppering the headlights. The storm appeared to be growing in strength. It was hard to see far ahead. He clutched the wheel tight. Beside him, Camo sat watching the familiar path.

"Almost home, boy," he said as he had through all the trips up the mountain he'd made with Camo.

The dog cast those soulful eyes his way. Every time Axel looked into them, he saw the battles Camo had fought for his country.

Axel edged around the last curve in the road. His place sat dark against the stormy backdrop.

He hadn't bothered with leaving lights on because he'd been certain he'd be back before the weather moved in.

He shook his head. He'd grown up in Colorado and was used to the weather in higher elevations. He knew storms could pop up quickly and it was best to be prepared.

The headlights spanned the cabin. Nothing foreboding appeared.

He parked as close as he could. "Hang on, I'll get the place unlocked and the lights on." Her huge eyes found him. She didn't want to be alone. "Why don't you and Camo come with me?"

He got out and went around to her side, opening the door. Axel held out his hand for her. Summer hesitated for a long moment before she clasped it and stepped from the truck. Once more her pregnancy reminded him that they'd be at a disadvantage if they had to escape on foot.

He quickly unlocked the door and ushered her inside, flipping on the lights.

The dying fire in the woodstove had burned down to embers. "Come in and get comfortable." He tossed some firewood on the embers and added crumpled paper until the fire caught.

"I need to check on the Jeep to make sure it's ready in

case we need to leave quickly," he said once she'd slipped into the rocker near the fire. Axel brought her some socks and a blanket to warm her up. She understood what he hadn't said. In case the men coming after them found Axel's house.

"But first, I need to try and reach the sheriff."

"No, please, you can't," she said a little too quickly.

"Why not?" He had to know why she refused to go to the police for help.

"He told me he has people in law enforcement." Her huge eyes found his.

Axel had met the sheriff and several of his people. His good friend Brayden was on the force. He didn't believe any of them were on the take.

Her gaze pleaded with him. "Please, Axel. You can't."

By not reaching out for help, it would be just them, and he wasn't sure he could protect her against so many.

"All right. For now, I won't call them, but if it comes to it, we may not have a choice."

She dropped her hand. "Thank you."

"I'll carry in the groceries and then change the tire." He hesitated. "And then I really need you to tell me what's going on."

Her expression grew suspicious immediately.

"Summer, I want to protect you. To do so, I must know what we're up against."

She held his gaze for the longest time before she nodded. "Okay, we'll talk."

He smiled. At least he'd won a small battle.

Axel headed outside and brought in the couple of bags in the back seat. He reentered the house, saying, "As soon as I return, I'll make us something to eat."

Summer didn't answer and he stepped outside into the storm once more. The howling wind made it hard to hear anything at all. He returned to the driver's seat and pulled the truck into the barn he used to house the cows and horses in bad weather.

After he'd made sure the Jeep was ready for travel, Axel moved it around behind the house, then fed and watered the animals. While in the barn, he changed the destroyed tire on the truck.

For reasons he couldn't explain, his gut warned him to keep the truck inside the barn, which wasn't its normal spot. Though it was a tight fit, the cows had room to move about. He checked on the horses again before stepping out into weather that was getting worse by the minute.

Axel started for the house when a sound that seemed out of place caught his attention. He listened but didn't hear it again. The wind?

After what happened, he couldn't accept it was anything as simple. He didn't believe the attackers' cars would make it up his mountain road but still, they were determined and would find a way if they realized this was where he'd taken Summer.

He couldn't go back inside without checking things out. Axel grabbed the old coat he kept in the barn and put it on. Treading carefully, he headed down the mountain while slipping and sliding at times.

As he walked, he heard the noise again. An engine! Fear quickly weaved through him. Just someone innocently driving down the road that intersected with his drive? Before tonight, he wouldn't have given it much thought.

He eased farther down until he could see the county road. Headlights crawled along it. Despite the storm, the passenger window was down, and someone flashed a light around. They were searching. Axel ducked behind a tree to keep from being spotted. The car hesitated at his driveway opening and Axel prayed the weather had covered up their earlier tracks.

He held his breath. Inside the car, snatches of conversation came his way. One name had him frozen in place. His name. Whoever these people were, they had the capability of running his plates and had found out his name…like someone in law enforcement might do. Was Summer right about not trusting the cops? If that was true, who could they go to for help… No one. They were on their own.

FOUR

Summer kept watch on the door as the minutes ticked by. So far, she'd counted off fifteen of them and still no sign of Axel. All sorts of dreadful scenarios flew through her head. Had Ray's people found him? Or worse yet, what if Axel wasn't the nice man he appeared to be? What if he worked for Ray.

She clutched the knife she'd brought with her in one hand and the armrest with the other, ready to spring into action at the slightest sign something was off. No matter what, she wouldn't let Ray take her again. He'd make an example out of her for all those other girls. And the evidence she believed she had on him would remain hidden in the walls of that old house. She wouldn't let Ray win. He'd taken enough. Summer thought about the other girls. She was so worried about them. Were they safe? Somehow, she had to survive in order to save them and future victims.

She touched her midsection. "I love you, baby." Summer had no idea if she was having a girl or a boy. Yet, she'd gotten into the habit of referring to the baby as a girl. Seeing a doctor had been forbidden. They ask too many questions according to Ray.

An unfamiliar noise outside captured her attention. She sucked in a breath and shot from her seat. Camo, who had been lying at her feet peacefully, did the same. His attention pivoted from her startled face to the door. A second later, he lay back down in front of the fire. Surely the dog would be more worried if there were trouble coming.

She went over to the window but hesitated. If she opened the curtains, looked out and saw Ray, she'd fall apart. But she had to be brave for the baby. Easier said than done.

Killing the lights, Summer inched the curtains apart. Snow mixed with sleet peppered the window. Nothing beyond the weather could be seen. Summer blew out a breath. The storm was getting worse. So far, Axel had offered only kindness. Should she go look for him?

The dog whimpered. She swung toward him quickly. Camo watched her with those keen eyes. Axel told her he'd once been part of the military. She couldn't imagine the things Camo had seen during his time there. But he wasn't concerned about his master. Perhaps she shouldn't be either.

"Okay. I trust you, boy." She flipped on the lights and returned to her seat, still clutching the knife. The dog licked her hand as if to say thank you.

"You're a good dog," Summer said with a little laugh. She rocked back and forth, the chair making a faint squeaking sound that seemed to be in sync with her heartbeat.

The wind outside howled like a wild animal trying to break into the house…or something far worse.

"He's not out there. You're free," she whispered to herself. "You're free." And she was. At least for the moment.

She glanced around the simple room that gave little away about its owner. Only the barest of furniture in the living room. A sofa and two rockers. The woodstove. And a chest in the corner of the room. It reminded her of the one in the living room of her home in Ohio. *Mamm* had a chest just like it where she kept their handmade quilts.

Looking over her shoulder, she saw that a small dining room led into the dark kitchen. She couldn't make out much about it. She leaned forward and peered down the hall where a couple of doors led to other rooms.

Axel Sterling had chosen to live a simple life isolated from most human contact for a reason. What was that reason? His only companion appeared to be Camo. She sensed he was trying to escape his own kind of nightmares. If that were true, they had something in common.

A breath escaped her, drawing Camo's attention. Despite her worries, the dog made her happy. "It's okay, Camo. I'm just curious about your friend."

The dog grumbled before settling back into his position.

The baby kicked and she grabbed her belly. Her child was active. When she wasn't waking her up in the middle of the night with movement she was stomping on her bladder. Like now.

"There, there, little one. Everything's going to be okay."

Eventually the baby settled down. Summer closed her eyes. She'd just rest for a moment until Axel returned. The wind continued to do its damage outside but soon became background sounds to memories of the farm and a simpler life.

At times, especially at night, she'd go there in her memories when things became too fearful. She could almost see her *daed's* face. *Mamm* and her *bruders* smiling around the table as they shared a meal together. *Daed* praying silently over their food. Both *bruders* roughhousing and sometimes kicking each other under the table. Summer trying to shush them…

The door flew open. Summer shot up from her chair, the knife poised as a weapon, eyes wild.

Axel stood in the open space, watching her wield the knife.

She sank back down, relieved, a heavy breath shooting through her body.

"Sorry, I didn't mean to startle you," Axel said. "The wind blew the door from my grasp."

She willed her heartbeat to return to normal. "No, it's okay. You didn't..." But he had and the tremor in her voice mocked her words.

"Are you warm enough?" he asked, ignoring the knife. The concern written on his face seemed genuine. He removed his coat and crossed to the trunk. Axel pulled out a quilt that reminded her of the many she'd helped her *mamm* complete. He placed it gently around her shoulders.

"Thank you." She did her best not to flinch when his fingers brushed her shoulder.

Axel slipped into the rocker beside her and petted Camo absently.

The frown on his face had her worried. "Something happened," she said.

He sat back and turned his face toward her. "Yes. I went down to the county road."

Summer's grip tightened on the arms of the rocker while she waited and prayed their location hadn't been exposed.

"There was a car out there," Axel continued. He told her about the window being down and the light searching. "They mentioned my name, Summer. They obviously ran my plates and know that I live somewhere down this way. But with the weather and the fact that I don't have a mailbox at the edge of my property, well, I don't think they'll be able to find us."

But she could tell he wasn't sure. He couldn't give her the guarantees she craved. Could they take that chance? "What if they do. Maybe we should leave."

His intense blue eyes skimmed over her face. "The storm's

intensifying. A car like that won't be able to make it up the drive. They left and I waited to make sure they didn't come back. Chances are, they'll wait out the storm somewhere safe. It may not break until morning. We should be safe until then. It will give us time to figure out what to do next."

She wished she could believe his assurances. "What happens if we need to make a run for it? How will we get away?" She inadvertently clutched her swollen middle. The baby. She had to think about her child above everything else. If Axel's answer wasn't good enough, she'd find another way herself. The cost of going back to Ray was too great.

He slowly smiled. "I have a four-wheel-drive Jeep with snow chains parked out back. It can get us through anything." Axel hesitated and she believed she knew what he would say. "My good friend is a deputy. I know the sheriff and many of his people and I have to tell you, they're all good as they get. They aren't corrupt, Summer."

She twisted her hands together. "I can't take that chance. Ray told me he had cops on his payroll. Cops as in plural. I'm sorry, I can't."

He slowly nodded. "All right, but to help you, I need to know what I'm up against."

Telling her story aloud would mean disclosing the whole ugly truth about how she was the one who had fallen for Ray's lies.

"Summer, whatever it is, none of it is your fault."

She clenched her hands into fists until she felt her nails biting into her palms. "But it is." She glanced his way and knew she had his full attention.

"Please tell me what happened to you," he said quietly.

She pulled in a breath and told him about how she had met Ray and how he'd made her believe she was special. "He asked me to run away with him." Summer couldn't believe she'd acted so recklessly. "I thought I loved him, and I believed he loved me, too."

"But he didn't."

Her mouth twisted. "No, he didn't. As soon as he got me away from everyone I knew, it became clear what was expected of me, and it had nothing to do with love."

The terrible things she'd been forced to do made her feel unclean.

Axel's expression was intense. "He's a human trafficker."

Summer hated those words. "Yes. He took me and several other girls to a house and forced us to do things for money. He told us if we ever left, he'd kill us." Thinking about that time and the innocent young woman she'd been back then had her fighting back tears once more. It was difficult sharing her story for the first time with anyone. It made her feel vulnerable. Would he judge her? See her as less-than?

The look on Axel's face held nothing but compassion.

Summer gathered the courage to tell him about the girls who had disappeared. "He used to brag about how he'd buried them where no one would ever find them."

A look of disgust crossed Axel's face. "What happened when he realized you were pregnant?"

Ray had allowed her a certain amount of freedom in her roll of working for his organization. She took care of the girls. Eventually, she even handled the books for him.

She shared Ray's plans to sell their child. "I had to fight for my baby." Summer looked down at her belly and told Axel how she'd waited until just the right moment when Ray was sleeping. Ray was a night owl and stayed up until early in the morning. When he'd finally fallen asleep it was right around dawn. She'd slipped out of the house with plans to get as far away as possible before he noticed "I was so afraid he'd catch me before I got away," she said once she'd finished.

"You're very brave, Summer," he told her with what sounded like admiration. "I can't imagine what you've been forced to go through. I want you to know, you're not alone anymore. And I promise I'll do whatever I can to protect you from this Ray and his people. I hope that you'll trust me to know when we need to reach out to the sheriff."

She looked into his eyes and realized every single one of his words were true. "I do trust you." Her faith in him was a surprise. She'd long ago stopped trusting anyone. But he'd listened to her story—one she'd never told anyone—and hadn't found her lacking. He wanted to help. And she found she wanted to let him.

He slowly smiled. "Good. I'll check down the road again soon. In the meantime, you need something good to eat." He rose and started for the dark kitchen. For reasons she couldn't explain, she didn't want to be alone. Summer followed him into the kitchen while Camo padded after them.

He didn't question why she'd come. Just pointed to the table. "Make yourself comfortable. How about eggs, bacon and biscuits?"

She couldn't remember the last time she'd had anything substantial to eat. Before she ran away, the food supply at the house was almost nonexistent. Ray hadn't sent anyone to do the shopping in days. Her final meal there had consisted of a sandwich, some chips and water.

"That sounds nice. I can help."

He barely let her finish before he shook his head. "I've got this. You stay off your feet. You've done enough running around lately."

Summer settled into a chair. She wasn't used to kindness. It naturally made her a little suspicious.

"I'm not much of a chef," Axel said. "Usually, it's something simple like breakfast or the occasional steak or burger."

Real food sounded wonderful. She closed her eyes. A pan clanged, causing her to startle. Would there ever be a time where she could be at peace? As long as she was running from Ray, it would be impossible.

Soon, the aromas reminded her of the hours that had passed since she'd eaten that last handful of chips.

She'd been walking for hours when she'd finally stopped to rest and had fallen asleep under that tree only to awaken to the storm. She'd waisted hours of daylight by sleeping.

When Axel had picked her up it was late afternoon, yet the storm made it appear like night. She and Axel had spent hours trying to escape Ray's people before arriving at his home. It had to be close to ten by now.

Fresh-brewed coffee teased her senses. Ray hated coffee and wouldn't allow it in the house where they stayed. Most meals were prepared by Summer. After she'd aged out, she'd been allowed to eat meals with Ray and his men.

She tried to recall the last time she'd had coffee. Probably before she left the farm.

"Food's ready. I know it's not morning, but I hope you like breakfast. It's kind of what I'm good at fixing." The sound of Axel's voice, so unexpected, had her jerking toward it. "Sorry, I didn't mean to startle you."

She hated being so jumpy. "No, It's okay." Summer stopped and drew in a breath. Once more, she struggled to free herself of Ray's influence. He was always there in her head, reminding her of the violence he could do.

At this moment, she was safe. Summer held on to that. She rose clumsily to her feet. At this late stage in her pregnancy, doing anything was hard.

"I'd like to wash my hands."

He pointed to the sink where there was soap and paper towels nearby. Though Summer had never been to a doctor, she calculated this to be late in her eighth month of pregnancy. More than anything she wished she had her *mamm* close to guide her through what was coming.

Axel stepped back to let her pass by as she returned to the table that looked handmade and well-worn.

"Do you want coffee…sorry, I'm not sure if you can drink coffee."

She hadn't been around too many women who were pregnant in the past. Summer had still been a child herself when her *bruders* came along one year after the other. She'd done her best to avoid caffeine during her pregnancy but occasionally slipped up when Ray brought home sodas.

"How about water instead." Axel went over to a cabinet and brought out a glass filling it from the sink.

"Thank you." She accepted the glass from him and pulled out the closest chair.

Axel poured himself some coffee and then brought over two plates before sitting across from her.

"Do you mind if we pray?" he asked with a little uncertainty.

She nodded without words. Prayers at her family home consisted of the silent prayer at meals. *Daed* ending it with an amen. Summer would pray for wisdom for the future while lying in her bed at night. Her father always ended their Bible studies with a prayer.

Axel bowed his head and closed his eyes. "Father, thank You. For allowing me to help Summer. For bringing us safely to my home. Protect us. Don't let those men find us again. Help Summer know she can trust me and help her to heal from what she's suffered. And, Father, protect her baby. Amen."

She quickly ducked her head when he opened his eyes. The prayer was a simple one and yet it brought tears to her eyes. Someone had prayed over her. She couldn't remember that ever happening before.

"Dig in. Oh, there's biscuits." Axel scraped back his chair and went over to the stove. He returned carrying a pan of warm biscuits. "Butter?"

She cleared her throat. "Yes, please." It felt strange having someone wait on her.

She buttered a biscuit and bit into it. The warmth and melted butter tasted delicious. It reminded her of *Mamm's* homemade buttermilk biscuits. She and her *bruders* would always sneak a couple while *Mamm* wasn't looking.

Soon Summer had polished off the biscuit and started on another.

The rumble of Axel's laughter drew her attention to his face. It was a handsome face. He had caring eyes. Dark blond hair that touched the collar of his sweater. He swept it back from his face often, almost as an unconscious gesture or perhaps a nervous habit. She certainly had her own ticks.

He smiled. It embodied kindness—a trait she'd almost forgotten existed. "I'll take a second serving as a compliment to my biscuit making skills."

She swallowed. "They're very good." Summer wiped her hands and then tucked into the eggs and bacon.

Camo nudged at her leg making his presence known. He looked up at her with a hopeful expression and she smiled.

"He loves bacon," Axel said. "Don't worry, boy. I have a few pieces for you." He set a bacon strip on the floor near the dog, who wolfed it down. "Pace yourself, my friend."

"He's a good dog."

Axel's attention returned to Summer. Those startling

blue eyes left her feeling a little unbalanced. "He *is* a good dog. He and I have kind of helped each other through a lot."

There were layers upon layers of unspoken emotions behind those words.

"How long have you lived here?" She and Axel had been through so much already, yet there was a lot about him she didn't know.

"A few years—since I left the service." His hands tightened into fists on the table, then slowly relaxed. There was a story behind that reaction. Axel had seen darkness, like her. "I bought it from the Amish family who lived here before. They got tired of the cold and moved to a warmer climate." He skimmed the room. "Personally, I love the cold and the isolation. It's peaceful."

Summer nodded then finished off her food without answering.

"Did you get enough to eat?"

She realized she'd been ravenous. Ray kept her fed but certainly not without hunger. "Yes, thank you."

Axel pushed back his plate and sipped his coffee.

She dropped her eyes to her empty plate. Axel had saved her life. Had protected her through several attacks that could have ended badly without Axel's skills. He had proven himself a good man. Still that little voice in the back of her head couldn't let her give her confidence completely. She'd made a life-altering mistake in trusting Ray. He'd said all the right words and made her feel as if she was the most important person in the world to him. And look how that had turned out.

His protective instincts increased every time he was eyewitness to the terror that seemed to have become part of who Summer was.

Axel's hands tightened around his coffee cup. When he thought about what she'd undoubtedly been through at the hands of the man she called Ray, all the anger he thought he'd buried with the man he'd once been resurfaced. He wanted to do bad things to this person who'd caused Summer so much pain.

But that was the old Axel. Now he prayed and trusted God to fight his battles.

Since he'd moved to Montana, a lot had changed about him. He'd found God. Gave Him all the anger and bitterness that had infested his heart after losing the woman he loved, because Axel didn't know how to deal with it himself.

Erin's unit had been attacked by enemy combatants outside of Kabul. Erin and her entire unit had died. Then Axel's world had collapsed. At that time, he thought he had everything figured out when he realized he'd fallen in love with his childhood friend. He believed Erin felt the same way about him. They'd have a wonderful future together with a house full of kids.

"I'm so embarrassed..." The softest of whispered words came from across the table. The past and the anger went fleeing. Summer needed him.

"Why? This isn't your fault. None of it."

She glanced his way for half a second. "It is. *I* left with him."

He waited for her to continue. She'd said she'd been a young naive Amish woman who thought Ray loved her. He'd gotten her away from her family and those who could protect her...then the true monster came out.

Summer didn't look at him once. When she told him about how Ray and the rest of his goons had used violence and threats against her family to get Summer—and probably many other young women—to submit to their will, he understood why she feared Axel. It was how she'd react to any man.

Axel's jaw tightened. "I'm glad you managed to escape."

She lifted her head. "I couldn't have done it without you. They would have caught me and…"

The horror she'd gone through broke the ice away from his heart. Axel knew then this was only the beginning of what he'd do to keep her safe. No matter what, he'd fight for her because so many others had let her down.

"What about your family?" he asked. "I know you don't want to reach out to the sheriff, but I could take you home if you'd like… They love you and want you back, Summer."

She shook her head. "I can't."

He let the matter go for the moment. "Why don't you stretch out on the bed and get some rest. I'll finish up the dishes and then I'd like to take another look around outside."

Right away the distrust returned.

"There's a guest bedroom down the hall. You'll be safe there. If you'd like, you can get cleaned up."

She searched his face for the longest time. Probably looking for some hint that he wasn't going to turn into Ray.

"I would never hurt you, Summer. I might have an extra set of sweats you can use. They'll probably be too big for you, but at least they'll keep you warm."

She slowly let go of a breath and said tentatively, "That would be nice."

Axel was grateful for the small amount of trust he'd earned. It felt as if he'd overcome a huge hurdle.

"Great. I'll get them." He rose and went to his room to retrieve the sweats. Outside the window, the wind screamed its anger. The storm appeared to be picking up still. It would be impossible to hear anything coming up on the house. The thought made him uneasy. He would have no way of knowing if Ray and his people were close until they were right on top of the cabin.

Axel gathered himself. He didn't want to alarm Summer. He returned to the kitchen and handed her the clothing and a second pair of his socks. "I'll just check around outside."

"Wait." The panic in her voice stopped him dead.

"What is it?" His attention went to her stomach. He had no knowledge of how to deliver a baby. If it were her time, he'd have to try and get her to the hospital, and in the current weather conditions it wouldn't be easy.

"Do you mind waiting to leave until I'm finished cleaning up?"

Relieved, he assured her he would. "I'll be in the living room. Come on, Camo."

The dog followed. Axel added more wood to the fire against the chill that seemed to be permeating the house despite the blaze. He returned to the kitchen and cleared away the dishes.

Once the cleanup was finished, he slipped into his favorite rocker in front of the fire. His thoughts went over what Summer had told him about Ray.

His good friend Lainey was a victim of a human trafficking ring operating in the area a few years back. The county's own district attorney had been indicted along with a police officer Axel didn't know.

Summer believed Ray had police officers working for him now. Someone had run his plates and found out the general vicinity where he lived. If he did reach out to the sheriff's people, would he be leading Ray straight to them?

A short time later, Summer emerged wearing his old military sweats, her blond hair a darker shade from being wet.

"Thank you. I feel much better." She slipped into the rocker beside him.

"You're welcome. But you really should get some rest." He didn't want to tell her they might have to leave at a moment's notice.

"Is it okay if I stretch out on your sofa?"

She didn't completely trust him yet. "Sure. I'll leave Camo here to keep you company and I'll be back soon."

He rose and started for the door. Camo didn't argue when he told the dog to stay.

"I'm going to lock the door behind me," he told her. "I have a key I can use to get back inside in case you're sleeping." Axel put on his heavy coat and gloves, then slipped into his boots. He grabbed his flashlight and stepped out into the nightmare storm.

Blowing snow swirled all around him, chilling any exposed skin. Up on top of the mountain, the snow accumulation was much deeper, muffling sound further. He listened but it was impossible to hear anything, much less see more than his hand in front of his face.

The light didn't pick up anything that resembled footsteps but with the amount of snow and driving wind, any tracks would be quickly covered. Axel killed the light and went by his instincts alone. He trudged through the deep snow that had already accumulated.

Once he reached the bottom of his drive, which intersected with the road, Axel stepped out into it and clicked on the light. A set of tire tracks had him quickly switching off the flashlight. There was no way those were from earlier. Someone had been here recently.

Axel's heart thundered in his chest when he caught something over the screaming wind. An engine. A vehicle was moving this way. They were likely trying to pinpoint the location of his place. He prayed they hadn't yet.

He hurried back to the trees covering his property and ducked out of sight. The noise grew closer, yet there were no lights. The driver wasn't using any headlights. How were they staying on the road in this weather?

The hairs on the back of Axel's neck stood up. The car's occupants didn't want anyone to know they were coming. Worst-case scenarios played through his head.

The vehicle was now even with where Axel was hiding. He eased a little away from the spot, but with the storm it was impossible to make out anything about the car as it eased past.

On the right side of his property was the Bureau of Land Management, or BLM land. It was undeveloped and unused.

He started walking toward the fence line that separated his property from the BLM land to make sure the car had kept going. Axel climbed the fence onto the government land and headed toward the road again. Before he reached it, car doors slammed shut. Axel froze in place. Low murmurs whipped his way. Enough for him to realize the occupants of the car had been sent to find him and Summer.

His first thought was her safety. He had to get to her now.

Before he had the chance to slip back to his place, a flashlight beam homed in on him.

"There's someone out here!" a man yelled. A heartbeat later, gunshots lit up the space where the shooters were. Axel dropped to the ground and crawled to the closest tree coverage.

"Get him!" the same man shouted. "Don't let him get away."

Like it or not, he would probably be shot in the back

if he ran, and if he did manage to escape, he'd lead them straight to Summer.

Axel whipped out his handgun and fired in the direction of the shots. Someone screamed. He'd hit his mark. How many others were still out there?

"I'm shot. Help me!" the wounded man called to his partners.

"David, get Jim back to the car. We'll deal with this guy."

There were at least four men.

Axel eased forward to try and see what was coming. Another round of shots from at least two shooters had him ducking once more.

When he'd left Afghanistan, he thought he'd seen the last of battle but like it or not, he was going to have to take down these men—all of them—in order to protect Summer. Her story had been heartbreaking. The things that had been done to her…he couldn't let that happen again. Not matter what—no matter the cost—he'd protect her because she deserved someone who would fight for her.

More shots fired had him getting as close to the tree as he could. They were using the gunfire to keep him pinned down. He waited for the last of the shots to ring out and then fired toward one of the shooters. Another scream. Another perp had been hit.

Footsteps running away seemed to confirm the last shooter was retreating. What about the man he'd hit? Had Axel's shot been a kill shot? Why else would they leave a man behind?

He slipped from his coverage and rushed after the fleeing man. If they got away, they'd know where Summer was and send backup.

Through the storm he caught movement and fired. A yelp told him the man was hit. He didn't go down but returned fire forcing Axel to take cover. Once the shots ended, he left his coverage, but couldn't pick up the man's movements again in the storm.

A car door slammed shut. Seconds later, taillights penetrated the weather. Axel ran out into the road and aimed at the lights. Bullets tinged off the back. The car didn't slow down. They'd gotten away, which meant he and Summer wouldn't have long before Ray's people converged on his mountain.

Axel started back toward his cabin at a fast pace. Once he reached the spot where the shooting had taken place, he found the dead man. He'd been shot in the head. Axel searched the man's pockets, not surprised that he didn't have a cell phone on him. He pulled out the man's wallet. Barry Harper was the name on the driver's license. It didn't ring a bell. Axel knew all the deputy's names and a few of the local police. There was no badge on the man. The weapon was a Glock. Some law enforcement agencies used them.

With nothing else giving any answers, Axel stuck the man's wallet in his pocket and headed back to the fence. Perhaps Summer would know him. Right now, they were in trouble. With her not wanting to involve the police, it limited Axel to where he could turn for help.

As bad as he hated bringing this deadly situation to his friends, at this point, Axel didn't see any other option. If they could reach Abram and Lainey's place before their pursuers found them, they stood a chance of escaping.

Unfortunately, the trip down the mountain wouldn't be easy in the Jeep. A rough ride under normal circumstances, the weather would make it much more difficult. With Summer being pregnant, the trip would be filled with dangers. Still, he had no doubt those men would have called for more backup by now. He'd engaged them and they knew he and Summer were close by.

He climbed over the fence and started toward the house while every stray sound had him jerking toward it. How big was this organization that Summer had inadvertently gotten herself involved in? How was it connected to what had happened before?

Questions flew through his head without any valid answers.

He neared the house—the lights inside had always been a welcome sight in the past. Even though it was only him and Camo, they reminded him that this was his home. His little sanctuary up on the mountain.

He removed his glove and fished out the house key. The wisest thing was to get the sheriff on the sat phone and tell him everything.

That wasn't an option.

Axel slipped the key into the lock and opened the door. He hoped Summer had managed to get some sleep. As bad as he hated to wake her, there wasn't a choice. This location was compromised.

He stepped through the entrance. Camo made a sound and looked up from where he lay on the floor near where Summer was stretched out on the sofa. She appeared to be resting.

Axel closed the door and hurried over to her. As he neared, she became aware of him and sat up quickly. She had the steak knife in her hand again.

He stopped. "Hey, it's me."

Her panic slowly eased and she lowered the knife. "What's wrong?"

Axel told her about what he'd gone through. "We can't stay here. There's one man dead down there. Although I injured two of the three remaining, they got away. They know I'm the one who helped you. They'll come back with others."

Summer stumbled to her feet. "What do we do?"

He hated risking taking a pregnant woman through some of the most rugged mountainous country to reach a cabin on the other side, but there wasn't a choice.

"There's a place we can go." He reminded her about his Amish friends. "They have a small place on the other side of the mountain, and it will be some rough riding."

She clutched her belly. "I'll be okay."

He had serious doubts. Unfortunately, they were all out of choices. "We'll take the Jeep." Axel glanced around the living room. "I have an extra set of boots." The flip-flops wouldn't work. Axel retrieved the lined boots and gave them to her.

"I'll gather some supplies for the trip in case..." He didn't finish, but there was a good chance they might not make it if the weather continued this way.

He ran his hand through his hair, a habit he had when he was trying to work things out in his head. They'd need blankets for warmth and food just in case. "Stay close to the fire. I'll be right back."

He grabbed the sat phone from the drawer in the kitchen and stuck it in his pocket. If things got worse, he wouldn't have a choice. Whether Summer liked it or not, he was calling the sheriff.

He retrieved extra blankets from the closet and carried them out.

Summer turned as he entered the room. "Let me do something."

He hesitated—torn between wanting her to rest after her ordeal and needing her help.

"You can help me carry some food." He went to the kitchen with her and grabbed a couple of bags then loaded as much food as he could into them. Taking up the heavier ones, he handed Summer a couple of lighter ones.

"Here, use this coat." With his free hand, he gave her the warmest one and slipped on the second one he kept near the door before grabbing the blankets. "The Jeep is behind the house." He looked into her eyes. "Stay close to me. Come, Camo."

Axel opened the back door and stepped out into a storm that was far worse than before.

Camo realized where they were going and trotted out in front of them as Axel locked up. Though only a short distance from the house, it felt as if it took forever to reach the Jeep. Axel opened the door and ushered Summer inside and out of the weather. He quickly loaded the supplies in the back of the Jeep and let Camo hop in.

He didn't waste time getting behind the wheel. Axel started the Jeep and quickly reversed while hoping the driving snow would soon cover up their tracks.

Like it or not, he wouldn't have a choice but to use the headlights. The terrain summiting the mountain was going to be difficult enough to maneuver.

Soon the rocks that littered the place became more intense.

Summer grabbed the door handle. "Where are we going?" She shot him a suspicious look.

"I told you. To my friends' place. We can stay with them until we figure out our next move. They're good people."

"This is the couple who gave you Camo."

He nodded, glad she appeared less worried. Axel understood what she'd gone through made it hard to trust. He'd just have to find ways to show her that she could trust him.

"What if they come after us there?" she asked.

"Then we'll figure it out."

His attention returned to the nightmare in front of them as the Jeep climbed over rocks that were almost as big as it.

"The snow should cover our tracks," he assured her. "It's really blowing. If they come to the house, and I believe they will, there should be no way they'd know about the small Amish community down below." Axel prayed those words would prove true, but Summer had been kept in the area. It stood to reason that Ray was staying somewhere close by. How well did he know the part of the state in which he was hiding?

The lights of the house disappeared in the swirling snow. He'd done his best to make sure his place looked as if the owners had simply left for a visit or a trip to town.

Summer's attention was fixed on the obstacles in front of them while Axel did his best to avoid damaging the Jeep. If they got stuck up here, they could die long before Ray's people reached them.

Though he'd gone down this way to visit his friends many times in the past, it had never been in these conditions. Axel was worried. He couldn't keep from checking the rearview and side mirrors expecting danger to appear at any moment. He could just see hisdriveway off to his right. So far, no sign of the traffickers. They had a moment of reprieve that he didn't believe would last.

He prayed they'd summit and be heading down the mountain before those men discovered the way up to his house.

His hands tightened on the wheel. He needed something to take his mind off the danger they faced. Then Axel remembered the identity of the man he'd shot.

"Do you know a man by the name of Barry Harper?"

he asked and swung toward Summer. The look on her face was one of sheer terror. It was brutally clear she knew the man he'd killed. And she was afraid of him.

FIVE

Barry Harper. Hearing the name made her almost physically ill. Barry's cruel face would be imprinted in her brain forever. Just seeing him enter a room used to fill her with fear.

"You know him," Axel apparently deduced from her expression.

She swallowed several times before she found her voice. "Yes, I know him."

"He's dead. I shot him."

Her head jerked his way. He'd been forced to kill a man for her. "I'm sorry you had to do that." Yet her emotions were torn between knowing what he had to do was wrong and happy that the man who'd been capable of such cruelty was no longer able to hurt anyone else.

His expression softened. "I had to kill him to protect you, Summer. And from the look on your face, I can see he was a bad man."

She ducked her head, her blond hair covering her face. Barry was that and more. Ray had nicknamed Barry The Enforcer. When one of the girls tried to run away for the first time, Barry would hurt them, and Ray would force all the women to watch the cruelty to scare them into obedience.

"He works for Ray. And you're right, he's a very bad man." After she'd tried to escape the first time, Ray had taken pleasure in calling in Barry. The Enforcer had beat her so badly that she thought she would die. She'd been left with her wounds untreated for days until she'd finally gotten the strength to get up. Eat. The other girls did their best to protect her from Ray whenever he'd demand to know why Summer wasn't working. He'd raged at them and told them that every day she was feeling sorry for herself was a day that cost him money. Everything was about money with Ray.

As much as she'd wanted to try and escape again, the thought of what Barry had put her through kept her from doing it…until now.

Axel glanced her way. "How many others were part of Ray's organization?"

Summer had lost track of the ones who'd come in and out of Ray's life. "Many. More than a dozen at least that I know of."

His attention shot past her to something over her right shoulder.

Summer turned toward it. Two sets of headlights crawled around the mountainside heading up Axel's drive. Ray's people were homing in on their location.

Axel killed the lights immediately, plunging them into darkness.

"Let's hope they didn't see our headlights, otherwise they'll follow." He leaned forward. "I can't see anything." A tremor of apprehension entered his voice.

Summer kept her attention on the driveway. The headlights appeared to stop. "They're struggling to get up the mountainside." At least it was something. She watched as the two cars appeared to turn around. "Are they heading back down? Maybe they're giving up?" She looked with hope to Axel. He was anything but hopeful.

"I don't think so." Axel kept the Jeep's speed at a crawl. "We've reached the summit that's close to my place," he said with relief.

The Jeep started down at a steep incline. Though she wore a seat belt, she was forced forward at the direction the Jeep was going. "I can't see the lights anymore."

Axel braked sharply, jostling the occupants of the vehicle. Camo straightened himself and then barked his complaint.

"Sorry, buddy." Axel put the Jeep into Park. "I'm going to slip over to the driveway and see what they're up to." The mountain's summit was less than a quarter mile from his place. He shifted toward her. "I'll be right back."

It took everything inside her not to beg him to stay. Axel was doing his best to keep them alive.

He waited a second longer for her to say something. When she couldn't, he quietly opened the door and closed it gently. Camo groaned as if sensing his master was in danger.

"It's okay. He'll be okay." She petted the dog's head while looking in the direction Axel had left. She couldn't see anything through the blizzard.

Once more she counted off the seconds, the routine giving only a small amount of comfort. Camo placed his paws over the back of the seat and waited while Summer continued to mark off the seconds under her breath.

One, two, three…

The wind rocked the Jeep back and forth, further straining her taut nerves.

Ten, eleven, twelve…

Beyond the darkness and the embattled Jeep, she saw flashlights down the drive. Ray's cronies had abandoned their vehicles and were coming after them on foot.

"Hurry, Axel."

Every second they were standing still gave Ray a chance to find them.

Someone materialized near her side of the Jeep. Summer bit back a scream when she realized it was Axel.

He slipped into the Jeep and closed the door. "There's at least six men down there. Having to come in on foot will slow them down, but if they find the pickup, they might use it to pursue."

He put the Jeep into Drive and started downhill. "I'm hoping we're far enough down that they won't see the headlights because I'm driving blind here. I can't see anything."

Pulling in a breath, Axel flipped on the lights. The path in front of them was immediately illuminated. It was far worse than Summer imagined. Huge rocks littered the way.

Axel did his best to avoid most. The rest he ended up crawling the Jeep over.

"How far is your friends' place?" she asked while gripping the hand rest and the seat. The jarring of the vehicle made her nauseous.

"Maybe four miles. Are you holding up okay?" Axel's concern for her was clear.

She pulled in several breaths. The nausea subsided somewhat. "Yes, I think so." Four miles in these conditions? It could take hours to reach his friends.

She looked over her shoulder. The flashlights were no longer visible. "I don't see anyone coming after us."

"That's a good thing." He offered a half smile. "With the wind squalling, I don't think they'll hear the Jeep's engine." Axel leaned forward to scan the path in front of them. He continued dodging rocks until they began to thin away to be replaced by trees.

"I'd forgotten how hairy the trip down can be under

normal conditions and in the daylight. Everything okay?" Axel looked her way.

She managed a nod. Truth be told she was terrified. Of the weather—one false move could result in death. Of the people hunting them who appeared relentless in their pursuit. If they kept coming like this…

"What do you think will happen when they don't find us at your house?" she asked. "They'll know we've been there because of the woodstove." Even though Axel had done his best to extinguish the fire, it still smoldered.

"After what happened on BLM land, I'm hoping they think we fled the area using my driveway. It would make sense to me but…"

What about their tracks near the shed? Would the relentless snowstorm cover it up in time? As much as she wanted to believe Ray's people wouldn't search the property too closely, she knew Ray. Those who worked for him were as frightened of Ray as Summer was. They'd turn over every rock looking for her and Axel because having to tell Ray they'd escaped was not a solution. Ray required complete loyalty and he'd do whatever was necessary to protect his investment from the threat Summer posed. She knew so much about his organization. He'd thought her weak and easy to intimidate but he'd been wrong. She'd listened when he hadn't realized it and she had a good memory. Plus, there was enough on that thumb drive to put Ray and everyone in his organization in jail.

One of their conversations played through her mind. It happened when the other girls were out, and it was just the two of them. Ray got bored easily. On this particular occasion, he'd been pacing around the house with too much pent-up energy. He'd told her something that terrified her.

Ray had bragged about how much he enjoyed killing

people. She'd been horrified and yet he'd laughed at her shock. Ray had let something slip probably because he was certain she was too afraid of him to tell anyone. He'd said he'd killed lots of people when he was young. He got this creepy faraway look on his face as if he were reliving the kills. He'd told her how exciting it was to watch life slip from someone's body as you choked them. He'd been inches away from her, no doubt seeing the same fear in her as he had in his previous victims.

She thought she would die that day. And then he'd snapped out of it and been his normal self. For a long time after that, she was terrified she'd be his next victim.

"Looks like we've reached the bottom of the mountain." Axel sighed in relief. Through the headlights, tall trees appeared to grow thicker. They were entering a wooded area.

"Does your friend live in the woods?" Summer asked, the doubt returning to her tone. "I'm sorry… Eight years has made me jaded. I want to fix that before my child comes." She didn't want to pass on fear to the baby.

"It's okay. They live just past the trees actually. There's another mountain range beyond here. They live right before the foothills. There's a small Amish settlement with a handful of farms."

"We're close to Amish country." A glance her way confirmed she was struggling to hold onto her emotions. "Once Ray told me what was expected of me in the future, he moved me and a handful of other girls out west." A tiny smile touched her lips. "We passed many Amish buggies along the way. I couldn't take my eyes off them. I tried to memorize every detail of the life I'd been so willing to give up." She shrugged. "Through these nightmare years,

I can't tell you how often I've longed to return to the girl I'd been back then."

Her story broke his heart and he vowed he'd help her get back to her family someday. Maybe then, he'd be able to let go of the regret he still held onto because of Erin. Axel had hesitated to tell Erin how he felt about her. Would knowing about his love have made those final moments easier? He'd never know.

Once they reached the trees the storm seemed slightly more subdued.

Summer turned around in her seat. "No sign we've been followed."

Axel nodded. "I figure by now, even with this weather, they're almost at the house. I'd like to be through the woods when that happens." He couldn't keep the worried edge out of his voice.

"Will your friends be okay with us bringing our troubles to their doorstep? I don't want to bring shame to their family."

"Hey, no one's judging you, Summer. You didn't choose this way of life. It was forced on you."

She slowly nodded.

"Last year, something like this happened. Both Abram and his wife, Lainey, got sucked into the nightmare." He told her about how Lainey had been kidnapped by a man named Harley Owens who had proceeded to take a deputy hostage. "They almost died. Then Abram and his brother-in-law rescued them."

"That's awful."

"It was. Owens and Phillip Hollis, the county's district attorney, were involved along with a local cop." He glanced her way. "According to my friend, Brayden, who joined the sheriff's department after the incident, a thorough investigation confirmed there were never any other officers indicted." He said that to put her mind at ease.

"I recognize two of the names you mentioned. Ray met up with Harley Owens once, along with another man who tried to keep his identity a secret. A short time after the meeting, Harley and the other man—Phillip Hollis—were arrested along with part of Ray's crew. He was furious." She told him how Ray had been enraged for weeks afterward and had taken out his anger on everyone around him. He berated those who had landed in custody and had become paranoid that the police were closing in on him. He'd been forced to suspend his enterprise and move it to another location until the heat settled from the county.

"Ray said he had to take different precautions to prevent that from ever happening again. He tightened security. He didn't trust anyone he came in contact with."

Axel's hands tightened on the wheel. "That must have been horrible. What an evil human being."

"You don't know the half of it."

"I have no doubt." His mouth thinned. Ray deserved to be in jail.

"Most of the girls were so young," Summer said in a strangled voice. "I hated what they had to go through. They'd cry after their first initiation into the business, and I tried to quiet them. Ray hated tears. He said it showed weakness and he wasn't one to allow weakness. I'd do my best to keep them calm and assure them everything would be okay even though I knew it wouldn't." She told him many of the girls eventually gave in and accepted their fate. Others fought. For those it was the hardest. A few tried to run. They never returned.

Ray was a true monster preying on the innocent. How many lives had he ruined because of greed?

"Have you lived here in Montana all your life?" Summer asked, the question intruding into his dark thoughts.

"For several years now." Camo made a sound as he settled into his seat, and Axel glanced his way briefly. "I grew up in Colorado. It was just me and my parents, but it always felt like I was protected from everything. Joining the military really opened my eyes to the real world."

"I'd give anything to be able to go back to another time," Summer said earnestly.

He wished he could wipe away every bad thing Ray had done to her.

Lights appeared up ahead. "Those are from Abram's home." Summer focused on where he pointed. A tiny pin light was all that was visible through the storm.

She wrung her hands. "I really hate that we have to involve them."

"Trust me, Abram and Lainey are good people. They'll want to help." He told her about how Lainey had joined the Amish faith after what happened with the previous trafficking ring a few years back. She and Abram had wed and made a life together farming and helping animals in need.

"They sound nice."

"They don't judge," he said, sensing her concerns.

The woods had been cleared away as they drew closer to the house. As bad as what they'd gone through so far was, the thought of the unknowns that lay in front of them had Axel's stomach doing a somersault.

The barn appeared off to the right, then the house.

Summer swallowed as Axel stopped the Jeep in front.

He barely had time to park the vehicle before Abram stepped from the porch with a lantern held high. Worry on his face. He recognized the Jeep and smiled.

Axel waved and shifted to her. "Let me explain things

to them. Stay here with Camo where it's warm." She appeared grateful at his offer.

Axel shoved the door open against the wind and got out. It slammed shut before he could close it. He noticed Summer jump nervously.

He hurried up the steps and shook Abram's hand.

"What brings you out on a night like this, my friend?" Abram's joy at seeing Axel soon turned to concern. He glanced through the snow-covered window at Summer. The Amish man's brow creased. "Something has happened." When Axel struggled to find the words, he added, "Is it bad?"

"It's bad." Axel did his best to explain what Summer had gone through and what they'd battled so far. "We need a place to hide out and warm up. I'm sorry to have to bring this to you, Abram, but I didn't know where else to go."

Abram shook his head. "Nonsense. You did the right thing. Please, come inside."

"Thank you, my friend." Axel came around to Summer's side. He helped her out and held on to her arm when the wind would have blown her around. "Let's get you inside." As they headed for the porch, Axel scanned the snowy world around them and wondered how long they would have before they were found and forced into another battle Axel wasn't sure they could win.

SIX

Summer searched Axel's handsome face and wished she could erase the things that were forever imprinted in her heart, keeping her from experiencing anything close to a human emotion again. But she couldn't. She was damaged beyond repair.

He cleared his throat. "Are you okay?" The huskiness in his voice made her wonder what he was thinking.

She nodded because saying words seemed impossible.

"Come, Camo." The dog trotted up the porch steps.

Abram had opened the door and was standing in the threshold with a woman who appeared to be in her early twenties.

Camo ran past them into the house and the young woman laughed. "Please come inside and make yourself at home like Camo." She bunched her apron in her hands. "I'm Lainey and this is my husband, Abram."

"Summer." She hated the name because of all it represented.

"It's nice to meet you, Summer. Please, come in and sit by the fire." Lainey pointed to the warmth permeating from the woodstove.

"Thank you." Summer slipped into one of the chairs, her attention glued on Axel. Despite her hesitation to trust anyone, he made her feel safe.

"I should get the Jeep out of sight," Axel told her and immediately what little bit of progress she'd made at letting go of her fears evaporated.

He came over to where she sat and knelt beside her. "I'll be right back, I promise. In the meantime, you're safe here. Is it okay if I use the barn?" he asked Abram.

"*Jah*," Abram confirmed. "I'll come with you to get the doors."

"Thanks, Abram." Axel turned to her with eyes that held encouragement. "I won't be long."

When the two men stepped outside, Lainey brought over a quilt and placed it on Summer's lap. She slipped into the vacant chair.

"I'm glad you both made it safely. Abram told me Axel mentioned you were attacked?" Lainey's expression was kind. She was looking for answers Summer wasn't sure she could give.

"Yes. There are some bad men coming after me. Axel saved me." She swallowed. If only it was that simple. "They followed us to his house." Camo once more stuck his head in Summer's lap as if realizing she was struggling.

Lainey laughed at the dog's behavior. "He really likes you. Except for Axel, Camo doesn't normally warm up to others easily."

"He's been a *gut* watchdog." Summer smiled down at the dog and stroked his head.

"Are you Amish?" Lainey asked in surprise. Summer realized she'd slipped up.

"Not anymore." She looked at the other woman and saw sympathy there.

"I'm a new Amish believer myself. I'm still adjusting to the language difference. My *mann* and I met when something bad happened here a few years back. Through all the bad, *Gott* brought us together." She smiled warmly. "When is your baby due?"

"In another month I think." If Lainey considered it strange that Summer didn't know the exact time of her birth she didn't comment.

She held Summer's gaze. "It could have been me. What happened to you could have been me." The words were said so softly that she almost didn't catch them. But she understood. Lainey could have suffered the same fate as Summer.

She cleared her throat, but the tears refused to stay back. She covered her face with her hands.

"I'm so sorry that happened to you," Lainey said gently, "but you're safe here."

Summer scrubbed her face. "I'm not sure for how long. Ray's people are searching for us now." She sniffed several times. "How long before they come here."

"Those terrible men," Lainey muttered, her lips thinning. "I can't believe such awful things are still happening here in our county."

Summer blew out a shuddering sigh. "I'm sorry for bringing this to you and Abram."

Lainey shook her head. "*Nay*. You have nothing to apologize for. These men must be stopped. Did Axel call the sheriff?"

Immediately Summer's guard was up. "No, and we can't call them ever." She told Lainey about what Ray had said.

"I know in the past there was a police officer involved, but not the sheriff's men. I trust them. I have a *gut* friend who works for them, and I know Axel's friend Brayden does as well. You can trust them."

Before Summer could respond, Axel returned with Abram. He zeroed in on her face, no doubt seeing the turmoil there. "Everything good here?"

She did her best to reassure him it was, and he didn't press.

"The vehicle is secured for now." He pulled up another chair near her. "We need to try to reach the sheriff. It's time, Summer. We're safe for now, but I don't believe those men will give up. It's only a matter of time before they widen their search."

She shivered. Trusting Axel and Lainey, when they both assured her she could rely on the sheriff, was hard. Yet something in Lainey's story got to her. She had a friend who was on the force, too. Summer slowly nodded. "Okay."

He smiled and rose, pulling out the sat phone he'd brought with him. He dialed a number and waited. "Nothing but a fast busy signal." His gaze locked with Abram's. "Either the weather's preventing the call from going through or there are too many people trying to use the service."

An uneasy feeling coiled down into the pit of her stomach. They had no way of calling for help and there were armed men after them who wouldn't hesitate to take all of their lives.

Axel had never felt more helpless. He'd convinced Summer to call for help and now he couldn't get the call to go through.

"Maybe once the storm lets up," Abram said and clamped Axel's shoulder for encouragement.

Waiting didn't ease Axel's anxiety one little bit. Would they have that long?

"I could saddle the horse and ride over to Elk Ridge," Abram suggested. "They aren't looking for me."

Axel turned toward his friend while his tired brain worked out the details. "That might work, but I think it would be best if both you and Lainey went together in case..." He didn't finish. If the threat showed up here, he didn't want his friends to get caught in the cross fire of a gunfight.

"I understand." He looked to his wife, who was listening to the conversation. "I will get the buggy ready."

"Let me help." Axel started for the door, but Abram stopped him.

"No, my friend. You're exhausted. Stay and rest. That will do you better than assisting me. I'll be back in no time."

Lainey stood. "Would you like something to eat while we wait? I made Yumasetti casserole and bread for yesterday's meal. There's plenty."

"That's very kind of you, but not necessary. We ate at my place earlier," Axel told her.

"Well, if you get hungry later please help yourselves." She beamed at Axel. "*Komm* and sit for a while, Axel. Perhaps the phone service will return soon and none of this will be necessary."

The clock on the wall of the living room chimed the time. Just past midnight. Hours before daylight.

Despite his worries, Axel smiled at Lainey's use of the simple Pennsylvania Dutch word. She'd told him how difficult it was to learn it in order to become Amish.

"Nicely done," he told her as she disappeared into the kitchen.

Axel slipped into Lainey's vacated seat and tried not to show Summer his concern. "Are you warm enough?"

She nodded. "Your friends are nice. I like them."

He smiled. "I do, too. They've been good to me." He didn't elaborate on how he'd found comfort in the simple ways of the Amish. He'd helped Abram and Lainey with their growing family of animals. Life for them appeared simple even though he knew it wasn't. Abram had shared about the time when he and Lainey were taken hostage. It had left Lainey with nightmares for a long time. She'd found solace in helping him care for the animals.

He leaned his head against the back of the chair, his fingers drumming a staccato beat on the armrest. The desire to be doing something to prevent what he believed to be coming their way had been ingrained in him since his military days. Waiting wasn't something Axel was accustomed to.

He tried the phone again. When it didn't go through, he returned it to his pocket.

"Do you think they'll check this far down the mountain?" Summer kept her attention on his face. She'd see it if he lied.

"I'd say there's a strong likelihood."

The door opened suddenly, drawing both his and Summer's attention to the gust of wind and snow entering the house.

Abram forced the door closed against the storm. "We're all set."

Lainey came out of the kitchen wiping her hands on her apron. She reached for her cloak from the peg by the door and slipped it on.

Axel rose and helped Summer to her feet. "Please be careful, you two. These men are dangerous."

"Don't worry about us. We will be *oke*. Remember, they aren't looking for an Amish couple." Abram opened the door, and he and Lainey stepped out onto the porch. Axel and Summer followed them outside.

The storm hadn't eased one bit.

Abram held his wife's arm as they made their way to the enclosed buggy. He opened the door and assisted Lainey inside before turning back to them. "Stay safe and keep your eyes open."

Axel nodded. "We will try our best. If enemies show up, we won't have a choice. We'll have to leave."

"We will be praying for you." Abram climbed up into the buggy. A short time later, he guided it away.

Axel glanced around at the darkness. More than the cold had him shivering. "Let's go back inside." As soon as they entered, he locked the door, a gesture that didn't go unnoticed by Summer.

"How long will it take them to reach the sheriff's office?" Summer asked, rubbing her hands down her arms.

"Not long. Maybe an hour in these conditions."

"What's wrong?" She'd picked up on the anxiety he couldn't hide.

"Nothing. I'm just wondering if we should leave now instead of waiting for Abram and Lainey to reach the sheriff." He hesitated. "I have a friend who is former military and part of the sheriff's department. His place isn't far from here. If we can reach it…"

Axel tried to relax enough to come up with a clear plan, but it was hard.

"You don't think we should wait for Abram and Lainey to return?"

"Maybe—I'm not sure." He hated sounding so uncertain. "We'll see what happens. I don't want to be taken by surprise. If we're on the move, we stand a better chance at staying ahead of them."

Both returned to their places by the fire.

"We should pray." Axel felt the need to talk to God. He bowed his head. "We need Your help, Lord. We're running out of options. We need Your deliverance. Please give us the strength to get through what's coming and help me protect Summer and keep Abram and Lainey safe. Amen."

Axel lifted his eyes and found Summer watching him. Had she prayed, too? Did she hold to the faith of her people still? He could certainly understand if she had doubts after going through the horrible things she had.

"Yumasetti casserole was my *daed*'s favorite meal," Summer said softly, capturing his attention. "*Mamm* used to make it for him all the time."

Axel couldn't take his eyes off her. "How old are your brothers?"

"Peter would be eighteen now. Eli fifteen—fifteen. I can't believe my baby *bruder* is fifteen."

He was silent for a minute. "I have two younger sisters myself. Kim and Bridgette. They're all grown up now with families of their own. Yet most times, I still see them as those little girls who followed me around." He hesitated before saying, "After this is over, you need to see your family, Summer. They must be worried about you."

She didn't look at him. "I don't think I can. I hurt them badly. I ran away in the middle of the night and never even left them a note. They must have been so worried. I wonder if they ever tried to find me."

"I'm sure they did."

"I can't believe I chose Ray over my family, or that I ever believed he loved me and would take care of me."

Axel's jaw tightened. "He's good at manipulating young women into believing he cares about them."

"I wish I could go back in time and warn the younger me of what would come." She swiped at her eyes and his heart broke for her. How many times had he wished the same. Even if he couldn't have changed the outcome of what happened to Erin, he might have let her know how much he loved her.

Every noise outside set his nerves on edge. It felt like danger was breathing down their necks, and staying in one place for long was too risky.

"I'm going to take a look around and see if I can find a place where the phone will pick up service."

"Can I come with you?" Summer asked, surprising him.

He was worried something would happen to her that would cause harm to the baby. His first thought was to ask her to stay inside where it was safe and warm, but he remembered how strong she was. She'd gone through things some people could never understand and she was still fighting.

"I don't want to be alone…and I feel safe with you."

"Sure. We'll take Camo as well."

Axel walked with her to the door where their coats hung. He helped Summer into his oversize coat careful not to touch her. He'd sensed she didn't like to be touched and he could certainly understand.

He pushed his arms through his coat and zipped it up. "Take my cap. It will help keep your ears warm."

He handed her the camo-colored knit cap and watched her place it down low over her ears before pushing up the hood of the coat. He had an extra set of gloves in his coat and let her use them.

Once they were ready, Axel opened the door. Camo ran past him as he stepped out into the storm that wasn't showing any sign of letting up.

"Stay close to me," Axel said near her ear so she could hear. She nodded and they started toward the barn. It was impossible to hear anything. Ray's men could be right on top of them before he'd know.

Camo trotted off ahead. At the back of the barn, he tried to call out again. The call rang once and then dropped and he gripped it tight. Of all times for the sat phone not to be able to pick up service.

"It's not going to work, is it?"

He turned slightly to see her clearly. She didn't seem fearful like before but almost resigned.

"What if Ray's guys find us before the sheriff can help?"

Axel squashed his own doubts. "I'm not going to let that happen. We have options." He started walking again and she fell into step beside him. Still, Axel didn't like sitting still. They'd talked in the kitchen for a while, and enough time had passed for Abram and Lainey to have reached the sheriff's department by now. Would he be risking both their lives by waiting for help? The soldier in him screamed they needed to keep moving.

"But you're worried," Summer said, correctly reading his mood.

They reached the edge of the woods they'd gone through, and Camo kept in the lead. "I am. I think we need to leave, Summer. If we can reach Brayden's place, he has a police radio." Yet there was a lot of rugged countryside between them and Brayden's, which was only accessible by snowmobile in bad weather.

Brayden had lived in the Tobacco Root Mountains growing up and had told Axel all about them. He'd invited Axel to stay with him at this small cabin. A few days of peace and quiet in the mountains and Axel had been convinced this was the place for him. He'd used all his savings to buy the house and stake his claim to a piece of the Roots, as the locals called them.

Brayden's place was even more isolated than Axel's. He'd built his cabin on the property that had once belonged to his people. The old family homestead was just down the mountain from Brayden's newer place.

Though the house was accessible through a county road, it took almost twice as long to reach that road. Brayden had carved a four-wheel path down the side of the mountain and had a shed at the base of it. Sometimes, he kept his snowcat, which he used to keep the path clear, down there. Did Axel dare risk taking Summer up the mountain even in the snowcat?

A few more tries of the phone confirmed it would be useless trying to reach anyone who could assist.

As much as he wished Abram and Lainey had an extra buggy to keep them disguised, the couple only possessed the one they'd left in. Should he and Summer have to leave soon, they'd be forced to use the Jeep, which might bring them unwelcome attention by Ray's crew.

"I don't see anyone," Axel said. "But then again,with this weather it would be impossible. Let's head back inside."

He and Summer turned and started back toward the house. Camo had been investigating something near the barn. The dog was focused on the trees near the back. When Axel spotted the hackles on the back of Camo's coat standing at attention, he stopped abruptly.

Axel placed his finger over his lips and pointed to the animal. "Stay here," he whispered before slowly approaching the dog's location. As he neared, Camo growled, his teeth bared. Axel immediately retrieved his weapon from the pocket where he'd placed it in. He looked back to Summer and motioned her to go back to the house.

She hesitated, but eventually started toward it. He turned back toward Camo. The dog growled again and lunged for something.

Axel raced to assist his friend, thinking it might be a wild animal that had Camo so disturbed—until someone screamed as the dog chomped down on his leg.

It was a man dressed in a heavy dark jacket, his face obscured by a knit balaclava.

Before he had the chance to advance on the man, movement out of the corner of his eye had Axel whirling. Another person charged. Relying on his quick instincts, Axel whirled around, his weapon pointed at the assailant. The man stopped dead in his tracks.

"Take it easy, buddy," the stranger said. "We don't want any trouble. We just got turned around in the storm." He carried an assault rifle assuring Axel this man wasn't here because he was lost.

"Drop the weapon." Axel kept his weapon pointed at the intruder.

The man didn't make a move to comply. "Look, all we want is the woman. Summer."

Axel tried not to react. There was no doubt: these were members of the ring. "I said, drop the weapon."

The man slowly smiled. "I'm afraid I can't do that. Call your dog off before I shoot him."

Camo had the first man pinned to the ground and wasn't easing on his hold.

"Not going to happen," Axel said.

The man shifted slightly, his weapon now trained on Camo.

Axel wasn't about to let him hurt his dog. He covered the space between himself and the man before he had the chance to react and slammed the butt of the gun against the man's head hard enough to knock him unconscious immediately.

The assailant on the ground used his free leg to kick Camo off him. He grabbed his weapon, which had gotten lost in the attack, and aimed it straight at Axel.

Axel fired one shot striking the man's chest. He dropped without making a sound, but the noise of the gunshot echoed all around. If there were others close by, they'd hear it and come to investigate. Axel noticed someone running his way and he whipped the weapon out only to realize it was Summer.

"What happened?" she panted.

Axel lowered his gun and blew out a relieved breath before explaining. "I had to shoot one. The other's unconscious. There'll be others coming." He glanced down at the unconscious man. "I'll need to get him in the barn and tied up."

He reached for the man when a noise captured his attention. Hooves pounding the earth. Axel dropped the man and hurried to the front of the barn. The buggy Abram and Lainey had driven came to a quick stop.

Abram jumped out and helped his wife down. "There are armed men canvassing the road," his friend said. "They stopped us and asked questions. I believe they suspected something because they tried to pull me from the buggy. I managed to get away, but they fired on us as if they wanted to kill us. Still, I think we lost them. As we neared the property, we heard shots."

Axel explained what happened. "Summer and I are putting your lives in danger. We need to leave. Can you help me get him to the barn first?" He gestured to the unconscious man.

"*Jah*, I can."

Axel faced Summer. "Why don't you and Lainey go to the house where it's warm."

Lainey put her arm around Summer and ushered her inside, closing the door to keep the cold out.

Once the women were safe, Abram slung the shotgun he used for hunting over his shoulder. As an Amish man, Abram was a pacifist, but he'd also seen what bad men were capable of and he wouldn't hesitate to offer assistance to Axel.

Together, they got the unconscious man inside the barn as he came to and started yelling at the top of his lungs.

"Keep quiet," Axel warned but it didn't silence him any.

While Axel guarded him at gunpoint, Abram grabbed rope and secured his arms and legs to one of the stalls while the man kept a close watch on the dog. Axel suppressed a smile. Camo could be intimidating when needed.

"We'll have to gag him otherwise he'll keep alerting his people," Axel said.

"Use this." Abram handed him a handkerchief.

Once the man was silenced, they brought in the other man. Axel double-checked for a pulse that wasn't there. Killing had been part of his job in the past, but he'd tried to put that behind him. Unfortunately, bad guys didn't live by the same code of conduct.

"I need to get Summer and leave." He didn't want to think what might happen if Ray's people found them again and he wasn't able to fight them off.

SEVEN

Summer huddled next to Lainey as they listened. Nothing but the storm. Were Axel and Abram okay?

"I'm going to look for them." Summer started for the door when the baby kicked several times as if she, too, sensed the danger they were facing. She grabbed her stomach.

Lainey hurried to her side. "What's happening?"

"The baby is kicking. I'm fine."

"Still, you mustn't go out there. It could be dangerous for you and the child. Come and sit."

"No, I have to help him." Summer reached for the door handle. It twisted in her hand, and she jumped back.

Axel's attention landed on her. He stepped inside with Camo. The taut set of his face assured her more bad had happened.

"We need to leave. Now." He looked past her to Lainey. "Abram is bringing the buggy up to the front of the house. He's going to try a different route to reach Elk Ridge. You must go with him."

Lainey nodded. "What about supplies for you?"

Axel shook his head. "We brought some in case we couldn't reach the house." His attention returned to Summer once more. "The Jeep's just outside." He held out his hand to her.

Summer hugged Lainey tight before she stepped out with Axel.

They headed toward the Jeep with Camo staying close. Axel opened the passenger door for her, and she struggled inside. The added weight of the baby had her moving much slower these days.

Once she was safely inside, he shut the door and opened the back for Camo. The dog had gotten proficient in maneuvering in and out of vehicles as if accustomed to riding everywhere with Axel.

Axel climbed behind the wheel and turned to her. "This isn't going to be an easy trip." Fear shot through her body as he held her gaze. It was barely a new day and still hours before dawn. The trip so far had been dreadful. What else was in store for them?

Summer secured her seat belt and waited while he did the same before putting the Jeep into Drive. They started away from the farm. In the side mirror, Summer watched the lanterns from the house disappear.

"I can hardly see a thing," Axel muttered and leaned forward, his face close to the windshield. "The weather is deteriorating into all-out blizzard conditions."

She noticed the tension in his profile, the way he gripped the steering wheel and his knuckles turned white.

Her anxiety doubled. If someone accustomed to this type of weather was uneasy, then she should be as well.

They reached the edge of the property that had been cleared and bordered more woods.

"How many more of Ray's men do you think are out here in this weather?" She couldn't help but wonder why just two would have wandered so far from the rest.

Axel frowned. "I don't know. It seems kind of strange

that those two would be alone. How'd they get to the farm on foot?" He slowed as they traversed the dark woods.

Summer thought about what he'd said. It didn't seem likely they were part of the team searching Axel's house. And even if they were, they couldn't have walked all the way to the farm especially in the middle of a blizzard.

Axel stomped the brakes suddenly, throwing her forward against the seat belt. "Sorry," he apologized.

She saw what had caused the move. A huge tree had fallen over.

Axel backed up and nudged the vehicle around the obstacle.

"There's a road not far from Abram's place. It leads past the Amish community and then eventually to a county road..." He hesitated, his thoughts likely running along the same line as hers. "They couldn't have walked in from there. It's too far."

"Then where's their vehicle?"

His gaze locked with hers. "There could be more men waiting in the parked vehicle. We have to go back. Abram and Lainey are in danger."

He stopped the Jeep and reversed enough to where he could turn around in the narrow space afforded by the trees.

Summer held on while Axel picked up speed as best he could under the circumstances.

As they neared the Amish home, a rapid release of gunfire assured Summer they were too late.

Axel floored the gas pedal as they cleared the final trees. He flipped the lights on bright. "Get down low," he warned.

She caught a glimpse of several men advancing on the house. They were shooting at Abram. The Amish man quickly raced inside and slammed the door closed.

As the men heard the vehicle approaching, they whirled toward the Jeep and opened fire narrowly missing it.

Axel whipped the vehicle around the back of the house. He bailed out and ran up the steps. "Open up, Abram, it's me."

The door swung open. Abram's worry was clear on his face.

"You and Lainey come with us," Axel told him.

Abram nodded rapidly and turned toward his wife. Before they had the chance to leave the house, another round of gunfire took out the front windows of the house.

"Hurry, it's our only chance!" Axel grabbed Lainey's arm and ushered her into the Jeep while Abram followed. He carried his shotgun, further reinforcing the gravity of the situation. Abram would protect his family and friends from death no matter his beliefs.

As soon as the couple was inside, Axel raced the Jeep toward the woods at the back of the property. Behind them, armed men rushed around the corner.

"Get down!" Axel yelled. The occupants of the Jeep got out of sight while he managed to avoid a stray bullet. He killed the lights and plunged the vehicle into the woods while shots kept coming their way. "At least the engine hasn't been hit. We can't go to the county road. They'll have men there waiting. Brayden's place is the only option."

Camo growled as if ready to defend them no matter the personal cost.

"It's okay, buddy," Axel told the dog. "We should be far enough away so you can get up now."

Summer sat up in her seat and glanced back to where Lainey's terrified expression showed how difficult this was. "Our poor house," Lainey murmured.

Abram placed his arm around her shoulder. "It can be

repaired. I worry about Martha, our mare, though. She's out in this storm."

"I'm so sorry." Summer felt terrible. "This is all my fault."

"It isn't," Axel assured her. "None of this is on you."

Both Lainey and Abram nodded.

"You can't blame yourself for what criminals choose to do." Abram looked behind them. "I see flashlights and something else…perhaps car headlights."

"That must be the vehicle they used to get here." Axel watched the rearview mirror. "If that's the same one that came after Summer and me, then they're all cars. They won't be able to follow us far." He smiled over at her. "That's one thing we can be grateful for. They didn't plan on the storm when they came after you."

She tried to hold on to the hope that at least her captors couldn't follow.

"My *daed* will have heard the shots and come to investigate." In the rearview, Abram appeared concerned about his father's safety.

"Your father is a wise man," Axel assured him. "He will know that that many shots mean trouble and will stay put."

Summer couldn't bear it if someone innocent died.

She glanced in the side mirror. "I don't see the headlights anymore."

Axel checked behind them. "I'm guessing they realized their car wouldn't make it up this way. Unfortunately, they'll look for another route."

Summer's frown deepened. "Is there one?"

He looked her way. "There are dozens of small roads around these mountains. If they're familiar with the area, they could find a way to cut us off."

Summer sat back in her seat with an uneasy feeling settling around her. What started out as a flee to save her and her baby's lives had ended up involving three other people. People now in jeopardy simply because they'd tried to help. Now they were about to involve someone else. If Ray's men figured out where they were going, Brayden's life could be in danger…just like theirs.

Axel was grateful he had the wheel to hold on to because his hands shook. What had happened back there at Abram's place could have turned out much worse.

He stopped the Jeep, immediately garnering Summer's attention.

"I'm going to slip back to Abram's place and see what they're up to," he decided. "I'll be right back."

She shook her head. "No, we need to keep going. If they catch us…"

He did his best to reassure her. "I won't be long."

"Let me go with you." Abram leaned forward with a serious expression. "In case there's trouble."

As much as Axel didn't want to put his friend in further danger, the man was an excellent shot.

"Thank you, Abram."

He carefully opened the door and blocked Camo from going with them. "Stay, boy. Take care of Summer and Lainey." Camo whined his displeasure at being left behind before settling down next to Summer.

With Abram close, the two headed at a diagonal angle. After walking at a brisk pace for ten minutes, they covered the quarter of a mile to Abram's farm. As much as Axel was hoping their attackers had left the property and were searching for another way to head them off, it soon became clear they hadn't.

Armed men were everywhere around the property. The car that had attempted to follow was parked out back.

"What are they doing?" Abram whispered.

"I don't know." Axel watched the activity. They weren't showing any sign of leaving.

Axel struggled to make the right decision. He doubted Brayden would have heard the commotion from his place, especially with the storm.

He shifted to Abram. "I don't want to put you and Lainey in further danger. I'm going to circle close to the Amish community and drop you both off. From there, it's a straight shot to Brayden's if we head east."

Abram searched his face. "It's too dangerous for you and Summer to go it alone."

"We'll be okay." Axel couldn't put his friends in jeopardy any longer. "Maybe you can warn the community about the danger coming."

Abram reluctantly agreed. "I'll saddle one of my *daed*'s horses and take the backroads to Elk Ridge. Be careful, my friend. There are an awful lot of armed men roaming the countryside."

"I will. I just hope the gunmen don't happen upon the community." Had they gotten a good look at Abram earlier? If not, even if they managed to come across Abram's parents' place, there would be no way for them to know Abram was the one they'd fired upon.

As much as he wanted to protect Summer by having her stay with Abram's parents, Henry and Esther, if their pursuers searched the place and found her, everyone would be in danger and Summer would be dead.

"We should head back," Axel said and led the way to the Jeep. As soon as they were inside, he told Summer and Lainey the plan.

"Oh, Axel, I'm worried about you and Summer," Lainey exclaimed, her concern evident in her voice.

"We'll be careful," Axel assured her with more confidence than he felt. He put the Jeep into gear and kept going the way they were pointing for a while. It took all his driving skills to keep the vehicle from striking a tree.

Abram leaned close to his window. "You should be safe to turn toward the settlement now."

Axel guided the Jeep carefully around several trees before shifting their direction. His thoughts went a mile a minute as he maneuvered his way through the woods.

One thought kept popping into his head concerning the previous arrests for human trafficking. Close to a dozen had been taken into custody years back. Many had been sentenced already. The sheriff's department had believed they'd broken the back of the trafficking rings in Montana. They'd clearly underestimated the magnitude of this criminal enterprise. At this point, Sheriff McCallister and his people weren't looking for traffickers. Axel needed to figure out what details they had to understand exactly how this type of organization worked. Summer would have insight into the way Ray operated.

He glanced at her. "Summer, what else can you tell us about Ray's operation. Is he working with someone else?"

"Ray oversaw the entire operation in Montana. Harley Owens and Phillip Hollis worked for him, though it wasn't always that way. Ray started out recruiting girls, but over the past eight years since I've been with him, he's moved up. He doesn't get his hands dirty recruiting the girls anymore."

Lainey sucked in a breath. "Oh, I recognize both those names you mentioned." She reached for Abram's hand. "I will never forget those terrible men."

Axel couldn't imagine the things Lainey had suffered at the traffickers' hands. He frowned. "What do you know about Ray personally?" She didn't seem to understand what he meant, and he added, "I'm just wondering how someone like Ray got to be in charge of such an enormous operation."

She considered the question. "He told me he once lived in Montana with his family. He said he moved away after he graduated from college and went to work for an international organization."

This had Axel's attention right away. "What type of organization?" Was it possible Ray worked for a much larger trafficking ring?

"I don't know. All he said was he'd worked his way up quickly to be in a position of power. He was so proud of what he'd accomplished." Her lips twisted in apparent disgust. "Ray drove an expensive car and wore nice clothes. A watch that he told me cost thousands of dollars."

Ray's organization was likely part of a much bigger one. He doubted Ray controlled the entire operation himself. What if Summer had seen the real person in charge without realizing it. "Did you ever see anyone visit Ray that wasn't one of his employees?" If they could figure out who this person was, hopefully Sheriff McCallister could make an arrest.

She started to shake her head but then hesitated. "There were four men and a woman who came to the house we stayed in once right after the arrests." She stopped as if recalling the moment. "They had accents, and they all gave me the creeps."

Axel sat up straighter. A woman? "Do you know what type of accents?"

She thought about it for a moment. "I'm not certain—maybe Russian? They were all armed and the woman with them was in charge."

His blood ran cold. Was the trafficking ring in Montana associated with the Russian mafia? Who was this woman in charge?

"They were all very suspicious," Summer continued. "They shut the door to Ray's office, but not before I heard Ray mention the woman's name. Vitaliy. I'd never seen him look so worried before."

The name wasn't familiar, but Ray's reaction seemed to confirm Axel's suspicions. Vitaliy, the Russian boss, must be running the entire operation. It would make sense that the Russian mafia would be concerned following the arrests. Those who were picked up might talk to shave time off their sentences—especially Harley and Phillip. "If the mafia is involved in what's happening, then this is bad on so many levels. Ray's life is in danger if he lets you get away knowing the things you do about the organization. I'd say chances are they'll probably kill Ray once you're located."

Summer's fear was etched on her face and Axel's concern ratcheted up to a whole new level. What if he couldn't protect her? Letting Ray capture her again was unthinkable.

It felt as if it took forever to cover the distance to the Amish community. When the first lights could be seen, the relief he felt was physical.

Abram's father, Henry, lived not far from where they were now. His place was a little away from the other farms. For this, he was grateful.

The farm butted up against the woods, which would allow for plenty of coverage. Axel parked the Jeep in the trees and turned toward the back seat. "Can you go to your father and tell him what's happening? You and Lainey. We will wait here."

Abram agreed. He assisted his wife from the vehicle.

Axel rolled down his window.

"There's a good chance those men may come here."

Abram nodded. "Don't worry about us. Watch your backs. These are dangerous people."

Axel swallowed uneasily, feeling the weight of what lay ahead. Could he keep Summer safe against so many? “We will.”

Abram shook his hand and nodded to Summer. “I hope you will come visit us when the baby comes.”

Her eyes shone with emotion. “I'd like that.”

Abram stepped back and closed the door quietly. Axel backed out of the woods and headed toward the mountain where Brayden lived.

“Will they be safe?” Summer asked, her attention on the side mirror as she watched Abram return to the house.

“I hope so.” But he wasn't sure. He was worried for his friends. He'd met Henry and Esther many times. They were good people who'd gone out of their way to make Axel feel welcome.

His thoughts flew in a dozen different directions. The time on the Jeep's dash said it was almost three in the morning.

“You should try and get some sleep,” Axel urged. Brayden might still be awake when they arrived. His friend had told him many times about how difficult it was to sleep through the night even after being out of the military for a long time. Axel could relate. He struggled with the same issue. Too many bad things waited for him in his dreams.

Brayden had lost a lot to the war. His marriage to his college sweetheart had ended after he returned stateside. For anyone who hadn't gone through war, it was hard to understand.

“I'm too keyed up,” she told him. “You said your friend's a police officer?” The reluctance in Summer's tone was clear.

“He's a deputy for the sheriff's department. Brayden and I served together in the military. I'd trust him with my life. You can, too.”

A soft breath escaped her as doubts warred on her face. "I'm sorry. I wasn't always like this."

His heart went out to her. "Don't be. You've been through things that would break most people."

She swallowed and fought emotions that seemed close to the surface. "Thank you. For being there to save me. For understanding. I don't want to be this way for the rest of my life." Summer brushed her hand across her eyes. At that moment, he'd do everything within his power to make sure she survived Ray's reign of terror and had the chance at living a normal life.

He knew Summer saw herself as damaged goods. In his mind she was anything but. She was strong and courageous and beautiful on the inside and out.

"You won't," he said in a voice rough with things he hadn't felt in a while. Realizing he'd fallen in love with Erin had snuck up on him little by little. A lifetime of being there for each other. Sharing things he hadn't shared with anyone else had made him love her. But he'd lost her and for a time he'd thought he'd lost himself as well.

"In time, once this is all over and you no longer live in fear, you'll come back to yourself. And you have the baby to help you." The real Summer was in there somewhere. He wanted to know her.

Still, it would no doubt be difficult for her to move forward as a single parent. His mouth thinned. He thought about his own parents. He'd been ten when his dad had taken off and he'd never seen him again. For months afterward, he'd cried himself to sleep at night. The scariest time was when he'd stopped crying. He'd stuffed his feelings down deep and tried to pretend he didn't care that his father had not only left their mother but also Axel and his two sisters, Kim and Bridgette.

Erin had been there with him through it all. They'd joined the service together. Been sent to Afghanistan. As long as he had her to keep him level, he was okay.

Summer touched her belly. "I've been fighting so hard to escape Ray and live that I haven't really allowed myself to think about the future." She glanced lovingly down at the place where the child rested. "I don't have a home, a job—how am I going to take care of my baby? I can't go back to my family—not like this. I don't have anyone."

"You have me." He didn't hesitate to add, "You'll always have a place to stay and someone to lean on, Summer. Always."

The look of awe on her face made him feel as if he'd done the right thing. Made him always want to do the right thing for her.

Camo made a sound from the back seat almost as if to remind them he was there.

Axel chuckled. "Sorry, buddy, are we not giving you the attention you deserve?"

The dog grumbled again, and Axel petted his head.

For a while, it had been just him and Camo. They'd gotten good at reading each other. Camo had played a huge part in pulling Axel from the darkness he'd sunk into following Erin's death.

"I'm going to flip on the headlights," he said. "We'll be facing some precarious countryside up ahead."

Summer's attention returned to the windshield while Axel prayed this was the right decision. So far, it felt as if he'd made a lot of bad ones that had ended in close calls and putting innocent people in danger.

She blew out a breath. "Abram and Lainey have been through so much. I hate that their house has been damaged. It's just one more thing to be sorry for."

Axel wasn't about to let her blame that on herself. "No, Summer. That's not on you. Don't let him win."

She ducked her head. "It's hard. He told me I was worthless for so long—that no one else would ever want me."

"He lied," Axel said softly. "Ray lied."

While she continued to study his profile as if wondering what he meant, it took all of Axel's attention to focus on the path ahead.

The mountain where Brayden lived was over seven thousand feet high. The deep snow accumulation prevented Axel from being able to see the dangers that lay beneath.

Summer told him about her family's farm in Ohio. "Where we lived there weren't any mountains. The winters were hard, but we were always able to get to town for supplies." She turned toward him. "How do you do it?"

He'd talked to many people who asked him the same question. His sister Kim was among them whenever she brought his mom and her family for a visit. Axel couldn't explain but it was the very isolation of the place that made him feel at home.

He shrugged. "I guess I find it comforting. Just me and Camo taking care of each other." He looked her way and noticed a far-off look on her face.

"Actually, that sounds nice. I'd be okay with not having to run into anyone again…or at least not anyone I didn't want to." Her expression turned hard.

"I felt that way when I came here after leaving the service," he said gently. "I didn't want to be around anyone, and I blamed everyone for what happened to…"

Very few people knew about Erin's death. Brayden of course and his family.

"You lost someone you loved," she concluded.

He nodded. "Her name was Erin. We grew up together. I was going to ask her to marry me when she died."

"Oh, Axel, I'm so sorry."

He swallowed back the bitterness that always made an appearance whenever he thought about losing her.

"Thank you." He kept his eyes ahead. "Anyway, I went home to Colorado for a while but I didn't fit in and so when Brayden told me about this place…" He shrugged. "I've been here ever since." He rarely talked about Erin, but after everything they'd gone through together, he trusted Summer. Still, it left him feeling a little vulnerable talking about someone he'd once loved so much and lost.

The stretch of landscape up ahead was becoming more elevated. The Jeep climbed over rock after rock while Axel gripped the wheel and prayed they wouldn't tip over.

"We should be getting closer to where Brayden stores the snowcat, although it's hard to tell for certain. I've only been here a few times with him."

Summer leaned forward. "Is this his property?"

"Yes. He owns this area at the base of the mountain all the way up to his house and down to the left side."

"I see something up ahead." Summer pointed.

Axel squinted through the driving snow and saw it, too. "That's the shed for the snowcat."

Almost there. He could leave the Jeep parked inside and head up in the snowcat.

As they neared the shed, something seemed out of place. He stopped and shut off the lights.

"What's wrong?"

"The door is open… Brayden would never have left it like that."

Her rounded eyes met his. "Maybe he's inside."

That would be the logical assumption and yet nothing about what they'd gone through so far made sense.

"Wait for me here," he said. "Lock the doors and don't let anyone in."

"Axel, maybe we should turn back..."

He glanced behind them. Nothing. "We can't keep fighting the elements like this. We need help." He was concerned about Abram and Lainey and their family. Were they safe? The traffickers had proven ruthless in their pursuit of Summer. They wouldn't think twice about forcing innocent people to talk.

Axel looked her way and did his best not to show his concern. "I'm sure the wind blew the shed door open. But let me make sure."

Her troubled eyes held his for a long moment before she slowly nodded.

Axel slipped the handgun into his pocket and got out. He forced out a breath and eased toward the shed. As soon as he rounded it and looked through the opening his heart sank. The snowcat was missing. Had Brayden taken it into Elk Ridge after all?

He stepped inside and looked around. Normally, if Brayden worked a shift during bad weather such as this, he'd take the long way. It didn't make sense, but they had a bigger problem. He wasn't so sure the Jeep would make it up the mountain in these conditions.

Brayden did have a radio that was part of emergency services and if they could reach the cabin, Axel could use it to call in what was happening. It was their only choice.

He stepped out into the night and glanced back at the open door. Still, why would Brayden leave the door open? It was unlike him to do so.

With questions rattling round in his head, Axel returned to Summer and got in.

"The snowcat is gone," he told her and saw her fear return. He gave the only answer that made sense. "Brayden must have taken it into town." He explained about the radio. "If we can reach Brayden's place in the Jeep, we can call the sheriff."

Her attention was riveted on the looming mountain ahead.

"If I'm remembering correctly, there's a spot to the left that isn't quite so steep. We'll try that."

But finding it in these conditions wouldn't be easy. He'd only seen it a couple of times.

He buckled his seat belt, and they started forward. Axel flipped on the lights. Creeping up to the mountain base, he once more leaned forward and concentrated on what he could see in front of them.

"I think I see it." He slowed to give himself time to observe the area carefully. There were no landmarks visible now, but it looked like the right spot.

Axel eased toward the path. The first rocks of the mountain were difficult and had him wondering if he'd made a mistake.

The terrain jostled the Jeep as he crept over it. Summer braced herself as best as possible and watched the scene unfolding in front of them.

"Are you okay?"

She forced out a yes she clearly didn't feel.

Even with the snow chains, the mountain was more than the Jeep wanted. Several times, the vehicle slid backward when they encountered more ice than snow.

Summer bit back a scream as they slid sideways and slammed against a boulder.

Axel exhaled a shaky breath. “Sorry about that.” He glanced down at the boulder that was blocking his door from opening.

“Are we stuck?” Her fearful eyes searched his.

“I’m not sure.” He eased on the gas. The Jeep struggled to gain traction. After sliding backward, the rock scraped along the side of the hood. Axel eased onto the brakes until the vehicle came to a sideways stop when it connected with another boulder.

“Third times a charm,” he said lightly to ease her mind.

After a moment, she laughed. “That was scary.”

“Yeah.” He hesitated before trying again. The chains finally caught and they inched up the mountain and out of the icy spot.

He could still see the shed. The direction of the tracks for the snowcat troubled him. Brayden never used the vehicle anywhere except to clear a path for himself up the mountain.

“Something’s wrong, isn’t it?” Summer had picked up on his worries.

He blew out a breath. “It’s not like Brayden to use the snowcat to go to town. For one, the tracks can’t go on the paved road without tearing it up.”

Her brow creased. “Do you think Ray’s men took it?”

It made more sense. If they’d stumbled upon the snowcat and knew its purpose, they could use it to travel in the storm.

“Let’s keep going,” he answered. “The sooner we get to Brayden’s place and the radio, the better.”

Summer settled back against her seat while Axel tried to let go of his misgivings. The tracks weren’t leading up to Brayden’s place. But it would be okay. It had to be okay.

EIGHT

The slow climb up the mountain was nerve-wracking. For every few feet they climbed, the Jeep would hit another patch of ice and slide backward.

Out of the corner of her eye, Summer spotted a silhouette. "There's someone else here."

He jerked to where she pointed. "That looks like Brayden's snowmobile." It was still about a good hour away from daybreak and difficult to see. Summer couldn't believe the things she and Axel had gone through since he found her the previous afternoon. Her attention was glued on the vehicle moving their way at a fast pace.

Axel frowned and moved the Jeep behind another boulder and parked. "If it's Brayden, he may have heard the noise earlier despite the weather"

She started to get out, but he stopped her. "I need you to wait here. I'll be right back." He looked over his shoulder at Camo. "You stay with Summer, boy."

He looked to the snowmobile light and frowned. "That's an odd direction for Brayden to be coming from."

Axel tucked his handgun into his pocket and got out while a prayer for his safety raced through Summer's thoughts.

He eased to the next boulder and took cover but not before the snowmobile spotted him. Instead of his friend waving, the man on the snowmobile opened fire.

Summer screamed and ducked low. More shots followed. Axel was shooting at the snowmobile.

The exchange ended only to be followed by a crashing sound. Then there were no more shots.

Summer rose and tried to see what was going on. The snowmobile appeared to be on its side. She got out along with Camo. Both moved to where Axel now stood at full height.

"That's definitely not Brayden," he told her. "Wait here."

He eased toward the unconscious man with Camo standing guard near Summer. The snowmobile had struck a boulder hard enough to crush the front of the vehicle.

Axel checked for a pulse.

Camo growled and turned. Before Summer had the chance to see what had the dog spooked, Axel yelled, "Watch out!" and ran toward her.

She swung in time to see two men in a standoff with Camo. A larger vehicle with tracks stood just off to their left. The missing snowcat.

Axel raced past her as Camo engaged one man.

"Get him off me!" the embattled man yelled.

The second was caught between helping his partner and zeroing in on the threat Axel posed. He whipped his weapon around and prepared to shoot.

"Get down, Summer," Axel yelled, and she dropped to the snowy ground.

Gunshots pierced through the night, whizzing past her head.

The sound of a scuffle could be heard. Axel was battling the man who had shot him while Camo continued to fight the second person.

Summer had to do something. She jumped to her feet and ran toward the struggle.

Axel and the man were locked in hand-to-hand combat. The two fought for control of the weapon in the shooter's hand.

She found Axel's gun on the ground where he'd lost it. Though Summer had never fired a weapon before, she'd watched Ray many times when he'd hold one on her or one of the other women. When she had a clear shot at Axel's attacker, she put her finger on the trigger and aimed. She fired. The noise ricocheted around the countryside.

She opened her eyes and saw Axel's shock before her bullet struck the unidentified man in the forehead. He didn't have time to scream. He died instantly.

Before she could react to the knowledge she'd taken a life, another shot was fired. She whirled toward the second man, who was trying to kill Camo.

The dog had the man's arm in his mouth and wasn't letting go.

"Drop the weapon," Axel yelled with the deceased man's gun in hand.

Summer got a good look at the man's face and recognized him immediately. DT. One of Ray's inner circle.

The man shifted his weapon from Axel to Summer. Axel didn't hesitate. One shot and the guy was dead.

Reaction set in quickly. Summer dropped the weapon as if it burned. She'd killed a man.

Axel saw and reached her side. "No, don't go there, Summer. Those men were going to kill us. You did what you had to do."

She pulled in several breaths before slowly nodding. Having to be put in a situation where you had to take another life was awful, but Axel was right—there was no other choice.

Axel looked back at the dead men. "Let's get out of here. We'll take the snowcat. It should be safer." They started for the snowcat that was still running. Camo loped in front of them, unharmed. "I'll grab our supplies and then remove the key and battery from the Jeep. If more of the ring heads this way, I don't want them using the vehicle to come after us."

She started toward him. "Let me help you."

He shook his head and held the passenger door open for her and Camo. "Stay here where it's warm."

Once they were safely inside, he disappeared into the swirling storm.

Summer kept her eyes glued to the direction he'd gone. An eerie sense of being watched had her jerking toward the place where the men lay. The weather made it next to impossible to see anything. Nothing moved.

Just the residual effects of what we've gone through so far.

She struggled to keep from screaming when Axel appeared on her side carrying a battery and some of their supplies. "Got them," he said, then stopped when he noticed her expression. "Are you okay?"

She clasped her hands together and searched for calm before nodding. "But can we get out of here before someone else shows up."

He smiled gently. "Copy that." Axel stashed the supplies and battery behind their seats before getting in on the driver's side. He studied the instrument panel for a minute. "I've driven this thing before with Brayden, but it's been a while."

With his attention on the dash, Summer studied his profile and was grateful to this handsome man who had saved her.

Growing up, when she and Hannah would attend youth

singing, they'd talk about the young men in the group and which ones they thought were attractive. After Ray, well, she'd seen men as monsters.

But she didn't believe Axel was like those men. She'd witnessed his friendship with Abram and Lainey—the way he and his friends looked out for each other. And she'd seen his kindness toward her. The vehicle lurched forward, and they were on their way. Just traveling a few feet made it easy to see the difference in stability from the Jeep.

"Does your friend keep his snowmobile in the shed?" She'd seen inside the building. It didn't appear large enough to fit this snowcat as well as a snowmobile.

"Not that I recall." Axel's frown deepened. "But that was definitely Brayden's snowmobile." He glanced her way and forced a smile. "I'm sure it's like you said and he left the snowmobile down here."

But she could tell he didn't really believe that.

"Let's just get to Brayden's place and get help," Axel told her.

His attention went straight ahead as the snowcat eased along the snowy mountainside as if it weren't anything.

"How much farther?" she asked while absently stroking Camo's fur. Everything about this nightmare had stretched her nerves to the breaking point.

"Maybe another mile. It's hard to judge when you're going uphill."

Summer settled into her seat and tried to relax. They were almost there. Brayden had a way to reach the sheriff despite the storm. It was going to be okay.

For the first time, she let herself think about the future. Summer glanced down at her stomach. The baby. Her child was everything to her. She'd find a place for them.

"It'll be dawn soon. Although with this weather, it won't

make it much easier to see. Are you hungry?" he asked, his strong, sure voice penetrating her doubts.

She turned her head. "I'm okay for now."

"Once we reach Brayden's I'll make you something to eat." Something shifted in his eyes. "I'm sorry you've had to go through all of this."

The sincerity in his voice made her believe him. Axel wasn't like Ray or the others she'd known.

"It was my mistake. I left the life I loved because someone told me he cared about me. I brought shame on my family." She shook her head. "That's why I can't ever go back. I've hurt them so much." She turned away when the tears were close.

"You made a mistake," came his soft voice. "You were young and you trusted a man who lied to you—who used you. Don't blame yourself."

She wanted to believe him…

"What Ray did to you was horrible, inexcusable," he added. "But it wasn't your fault."

She slowly faced him. "Thank you, Axel." She knew his words weren't some magic fix-it-all. And she'd have years ahead of her to find a way to lay to rest what she'd gone through, but hearing someone else say it meant everything.

Ray had berated her. Told her she was worthless. That no one else would ever want her. Her self-esteem was empty. But when she looked into Axel's eyes, she didn't see any of those things. Only a man who believed in her worth. He'd proven himself trustworthy over and over again since they'd met by risking his life for her. Axel made her want to be the person he saw in her.

She was so beautiful. The thought hit him out of left field. Erin had occupied his thoughts for so long. Nothing else had found room in his heart or in his mind. Until now. But he couldn't deny that since he'd met Summer, she'd occupied all his thoughts. Hearing her story broke his heart. Knowing that she blamed herself made him want to tear apart her tormenter and everyone connected to him. How could any human being do such terrible things to another?

As the snowcat jostled over the precarious terrain he thought again about Brayden's snowmobile. Though his friend had two, it didn't make sense that Brayden would leave one in the shed. Brayden would never leave the machine out in the elements, especially if he knew there was a storm coming, and as a sheriff's deputy, he'd be aware of what was in the forecast.

If the second snowmobile wasn't at Brayden's place, then it was possible Ray's crew had been to the house. The thought was unsettling.

He shared his concerns with Summer.

Her grip on the door handle tightened. "Do you think we'll be walking into a trap?"

"We can't dismiss the possibility. I'm thinking they went to Brayden's earlier, perhaps in the Snowcat and searched it. I told you there is a way to reach it from one of the county roads but it's a long route and so far, all we've seen them driving is cars."

"Unless they walked in?"

"Perhaps, but it would be a long way." He struggled to untangle answers that were illusive due to lack of sleep and the frantic pace they'd been forced to endure.

"When we get closer to Brayden's place. I'll hike up to the house and check it out."

"I'm going with you."

"That's not a good idea. They could be there waiting."

She shook her head. "I'm going. Axel, this is all about me. You're in this mess because you helped me. I'm going."

He admired her courage, but he was worried about her and the baby. "All right," he said at last.

Camo seemed to realize they were discussing something important because his full attention was on the conversation.

"You can come with us, too, Camo." Axel assured the canine. "We'll need your skills to let us know if there's trouble."

The dog settled down with his head close to Summer's hand.

"He's really taken to you." He hesitated before adding, "I meant what I said earlier, Summer. I have plenty of room in the cabin. You have a place to stay as long as you want. You and the baby."

She appeared overwhelmed. "You don't even know me. How can you offer me a place to stay and—"

"Because I see who you are even though you don't. I see you and I trust you… I care about you."

He hadn't thought he would say that again to a woman.

She smiled into his eyes. "You are a special person, Axel. Thank you for helping me."

"Anytime." Their gazes held for a long moment. Feelings he thought were no longer part of his being formed a lump in his throat that wouldn't go away no matter how many times he tried to swallow them.

Erin's pretty face appeared in his mind's eye. He'd told her he had something important to tell her. She'd been eager to get together…

His mouth thinned.

How could he think of another woman when Erin had given so much?

He dropped his hand. If Summer thought it odd, she

didn't say so. She placed her hand on Camo and faced forward watching as he continued to plow the snowcat through the snow.

At times, Axel wasn't sure what was the hardest. Not being able to tell Erin how much she meant to him or declaring his love only to lose her.

"How long have you known Brayden?"

Summer's question pulled him back from the heartache. "Going on eight years now. We served together for five. I've been out of the service for three."

"It must be hard to adjust to civilian life." Summer was watching him. Her gaze flicked over his taut jaw. The way his hands tightened on the snowcat's wheel as he tried to find a way to explain the nightmare of adjusting to life beyond war.

"It was." Axel barely recognized his voice. "I watched many of my friends die over there..." And he'd taken lives. More than he could remember except in his dreams.

"I'm so sorry," she whispered sincerely. This woman who had gone through so much had compassion for him.

"I don't usually talk about it because it's hard. Maybe one day, I'll sit down and unload my heart." He tried to make light, but her empathy didn't go away.

"Maybe one day I will as well."

He dragged in several breaths and slowly nodded. Both he and Summer were survivors. They had scars that wouldn't go away easily.

"Maybe we can help each other heal," he whispered and watched as she shivered but didn't look away.

"I'd like that. I don't think I can do it on my own."

He didn't think he could either, but he wanted to try and get better...for her.

For the first time in a long time, his smile felt genuine.

He focused ahead and realized he had hope again yet he was facing a dangerous situation. So much was at stake. Summer's life and her baby's were on the line.

Glimpses of something unexpected grabbed his attention and he stopped the snowcat.

"What's wrong?" Summer asked, her attention going in the same direction as his. "Are those lights?"

"They are." Axel didn't like it. "If Brayden's home, he'd be sleeping. If he's at work, there's no way he'd leave the lights on."

"You think it's Ray?" She studied the landscape, and he struggled to give her an answer.

"Possibly. I think this is as far as we should go in the snowcat." He turned to her. "It will be difficult walking from here but if Ray's people are inside, advancing on foot will give us the element of surprise."

He held out the weapon he'd taken from one of their attackers and she immediately shook her head. "Just as a precaution in case."

She reluctantly accepted the gun from him.

Axel searched her face before opening the door. He got out, and Camo followed immediately. Axel rounded the machine and held out his hand to help her down.

She stood beside him, and he could feel her trembling.

"It's going to be okay," he said softly.

She looked up at him with huge eyes that tugged at his heart.

He pointed through the storm. "This way."

Axel stayed close to her side. She was also eight months pregnant after all and he was worried about the baby, too.

He caught glimpses of the lights from Brayden's house, and his breath came in short gasps. The adrenaline rush he'd felt many times during battle had his senses heightened.

Axel glanced down at his dog. Camo appeared to have fallen back on his military training. No more loping around exploring different things. His full attention was on the ground. The dog's keen senses had hit on a trail. The only question was who it belonged to.

They reached the first stand of pine trees that grew around the cabin. Brayden had chosen a place among the trees to build his home down the mountainside from where he'd grown up.

The place was powered by both solar and a generator. Axel had learned a lot about construction from his friend, who'd learned it from his father.

He eased closer to the edge of the small, wooded area that Brayden had left deliberately to block the wind. The house was lit up as if every light in the place was on.

"I don't like it," he said to himself before turning to Summer. "Let's check the garage." He pointed to the left at the detached structure Brayden had built.

With Summer close, all three headed for the garage. If Brayden was indeed home, then his vehicle would be parked inside. If not, it could mean two things: Brayden had left, or Ray's men had stolen the vehicle and the second snowmobile that Brayden owned like they had the previous one.

He reached the side of the garage where there was a small side door. Brayden never left it locked. Axel opened the door and went inside. He didn't have to flip on the overhead light to see Brayden's Blazer there.

He bent over with relief. "He's home. He must be getting ready to go to work."

He stepped outside and closed the door. "Let's get out of the weather."

They reached Brayden's front porch. The curtains were closed. Brayden rarely kept them that way.

He turned to Summer. "Wait here with Camo."

She nodded, picking up on his anxiety. Axel pointed to the side of the house where they'd be out of sight, and Summer moved to the cover.

Once he was certain they were safe, he eased along the porch to the front entrance. There was no way to see inside, and he had no idea what he would be walking into. If he walked in and found Brayden, it would be a huge relief.

His friend told him he usually locked the doors at night. Axel tried the door. It twisted freely in his hand. Immediately, Axel's hackles were up, and he had the handgun ready as he carefully stepped inside.

That no one shot at him was a welcome relief. "Brayden, are you here?"

Silence was the only answer. Axel stepped farther into the living room and took in what was before him. A dying fire in the woodstove. And a kitchen that showed no signs of Brayden preparing breakfast. Though Axel didn't know Brayden's work schedule, Brayden was generally up before dawn to start his day. And daybreak had begun to lighten the horizon despite the storm.

"Brayden, are you still asleep?" Axel eased toward the bedroom. The door stood open. The bed was empty but had been slept in recently. He went over and felt the mattress. Cold. Where was Brayden?

He knocked on the bathroom door thinking perhaps his friend had gotten sick. When there was no response, he entered the space. Empty as well. A search of the rest of the house proved something was wrong.

He hurried outside and brought Summer and Camo in.

Summer looked around the house, clearly realizing the owner was absent. "Where's your friend?"

"He's not here." Axel was worried and trying not to show

it. "I didn't check to see if the second snowmobile was in the garage. I'll be right back." He stepped outside and tried to get his thoughts together. Perhaps Brayden had had to leave in a hurry and hadn't bothered turning off lights. What Axel knew for certain was that Brayden had been asleep at one time but had gotten up. But what would give him cause to take the snowmobile over the Blazer that was equipped with snow chains and more than capable of covering the rough terrain that led to the county road?

The answer was he wouldn't have, unless he'd gone down the way Axel and Summer had come.

None of it made sense. Axel covered the rest of the way to the garage and opened the side door once more. As soon as he flipped the lights on, the dreadful truth slapped him in the face. The snowmobile was there.

They'd taken Brayden.

NINE

Summer paced the living room. She was worried about Axel.

Camo seemed to be mirroring her steps. She stopped and looked down at the dog. "He'll be okay, boy." She hugged Camo's neck. The dog stared up at her with troubled eyes. "Don't worry. Axel's got this."

As soon as the words were out, the sound of footsteps on the wooden porch had her jerking toward the door. She let Camo go and pulled the gun out of her pocket.

The door flew open, and her heart exploded in her chest. When Axel appeared, her relief was physical. He closed the door and bolted the lock.

"Is the snowmobile still in the garage?" She scanned his taut expression.

"Yes, but there's something else. The SUV's been tampered with and so has the snowmobile."

"They've been here." Her eyes held his. "What about your friend?"

The grim expression on his face assured her Axel was concerned. "He's missing." Axel's attention shifted from her to something beyond her right shoulder.

She turned as he hurried toward a desk that was set up on the opposite side from the woodstove. She followed him over.

He picked up a microphone that was detached from a machine.

"It's broken." He turned distraught eyes her way. "The police radio is broken."

There was no doubt in Summer's mind that Ray had ordered this. The only question was why? "I don't understand why Ray would come after your friend. He has nothing to do with me."

Axel was still holding the broken mic. "I'm guessing they came here looking for us and managed to catch Brayden sleeping. They took him by surprise before he had the chance to defend himself."

"But he's not here. They didn't…kill him."

Axel flinched at her words. "Maybe they figured he'd be able to help them in some way." He stared at the mic. "They're gone for now. If I can get the radio working again, I can call for help." He ran a hand through his hair. "Do you have any idea where they might have taken him? What about the house you escaped from? Can you find it again?"

Her stomach clenched. The thought of going back there made her sick but if it saved Brayden's life then she'd do it. "I think so. It's isolated. If Ray's men thought Brayden could help them locate us in some way, they might take him there to…" She couldn't say the word torture. Ray and his goons had perfected that art to force people to talk. She remembered the time some of the girls had run away. Ray captured one and had tormented her until she'd given up the location of the rest. And then she'd disappeared. The other girls never came back. Summer had no doubt Ray had killed all of them.

"Brayden's strong." Axel examined the radio. "They really did a number on this."

"What can I do to help?" She'd asked because she had to do something.

Axel turned to her with a gentle look. "Just rest. I know you're exhausted." He went over to the woodstove and added some logs and kindling to it. Soon the kindling caught, and the fire began to penetrate the cold. He pulled up the sofa close to the fire. "I'll see if I can make us something to eat and take another look at the radio." .Summer used the restroom and then returned to the living room. She stretched out and tried to shut down her mind enough to sleep but it was impossible.

She heard Axel moving around in the kitchen.

"Can't sleep?" he asked coming back in. He handed her a bowl filled with stew.

She stifled a yawn. "No, I can't. Too much on my mind."

"I get that. I checked the radio. It's a bust. I think they may have taken some part of it to keep anyone who found it from getting it to work and calling for help." He sat beside her. "In other words, us."

A disturbing thought occurred er. "Unless they weren't thinking of us but Brayden."

Axel's frown deepened. "I'm not following…"

"Maybe they came here thinking they'd gotten your address wrong, and that you lived here. They broke in, but Brayden managed to escape. They could be looking for him."

Axel shot from his seat. "If he's out there on foot, he's in danger." He paced the room while holding his injured shoulder. "I don't even know where to start looking for him. In this blizzard, he won't last long."

"We don't know for certain that's what happened," she reminded him. "Is there any place close where Brayden might go for help?"

"My place," he said and pulled a face. "Abram and the Amish community are closer but there are no phones."

"What should we do?" Summer had no idea where to go from here.

He turned toward the radio. "I'm praying Brayden was able to make it out of the house without being caught. Right now, we need the sheriff involved in this dangerous situation because we can only keep running for so long before we're found."

Summer couldn't hold back her frightened reaction.

He came back over and sat down beside her. "I'm guessing based on what they did to the radio, there's no way I can fix the Blazer or the snowmobile." He huffed out a breath. "There's only one thing I can think to do. Go back for the snowcat."

She had a feeling this was what he'd say but still the thought of hiking back to the machine wasn't a welcome one.

"I think the sooner we get going the better." Axel pulled out the sat phone and gave it a try. His frustration was clear. "It's not going through."

She slowly lumbered to her feet. The concern on his face for her made her feel special. Summer hadn't felt that way in a long time.

Axel rose beside her. Only inches separated them. "I'm sorry I have to take you with me, but I would be too worried leaving you here by yourself, even with Camo."

She didn't feel worthy of his concern. All the terrible things she'd been forced to do played through her head, assuring her she was dirty and no one would ever love her.

"I'll be okay." Her voice was barely a whisper, his attention on her face.

"You deserve someone to love you and treat you and your baby right."

She swallowed but the lump in her throat wouldn't go away. "I want to believe you."

He tucked her hair behind her ear in an unexpected gesture that had her sucking in a breath. Yet, for once she wasn't repelled by Axel's gentle touch.

"It will get better. There are people who can help. I can help. I want to."

She believed him. "I trust you, Axel. I don't trust anyone else."

"Thank you." He seemed moved by her admission. "Then let me help you through this. I won't leave your side."

She could get through just about anything as long as he was there.

"Right now, we have to get out of here. Those men are still on our tail and could be anywhere. They're good at disabling things. If we lose the snowcat…"

He didn't need to finish. They'd be on foot and subject to Ray's men as well as the weather. "I'm ready. I can make it," she said even though she wasn't so sure.

He looked at her with awe before going over to the door with Camo at his heels. Axel cracked it and looked out. Even if the threat was out there somewhere waiting, it would be impossible to see or hear them.

"Stay close to me," he told her, and she willingly agreed.

Summer slipped out beside him and closed the door. Fear-fueled adrenaline swept through her body replacing the exhaustion. She stayed so close to Axel that whenever he stopped, she bumped into him.

He eased toward the edge of the porch and then off it. Camo was right at his side.

Together, they started toward the woods once more. Every step scared the daylights out of her. Summer was relieved when they reached the trees, because it allowed some amount of coverage.

"Let's take a break," Axel suggested. "The cold makes it hard to catch your breath."

She was too busy sucking in air to answer. Eventually, her heart rate slowed and she could breathe normally.

"Ready?" he asked after they'd rested for a few minutes.

Summer wasn't anywhere close to being ready to start walking again but she had to be strong for Axel. He couldn't fight this battle alone. "Yes, I'm ready."

He searched her face before they began moving again. Fighting the wind made it seem as if they weren't making any progress at all. Each step was a battle. The howl of the wind through the trees overrode every other sound. Their pursuers could be right on top of them, and they'd never know it.

Although the skies had lightened now with dawn, the storm and the woods made it still difficult to see anything.

After stumbling several times, Axel looped his arm through hers to keep her steady. Even Camo seemed to be struggling.

"Let's stop for a second and catch our breath again," Axel said when he noticed Summer struggling even though they hadn't been moving long.

She huddled close to him, using a group of aspen trees for some protection from the biting wind.

"It's getting harder to see where we're going," Axel said close to her ear. "Our earlier tracks are covered up by fresh snow." He pointed straight ahead. "I think this is the way."

After they'd rested for a while longer, they started walking again. Through the snow, something caught Summer's attention. She stopped. "What is that?"

Axel focused on what she was seeing. "That's a light. It could be Brayden."

The light disappeared with the swirl of the storm. "Where'd it go?" She waited but it didn't return.

"Let's keep heading that way. If it's Brayden, he could be turned around in the storm as well."

Once they reached the place where the glow had been, they saw that the ground was cluttered with footprints. More than one set.

"That's not Brayden—or if it is, he's not alone." Axel frowned as he studied the prints. "I'm more worried about Ray's people. Let's see if we can get back on track for the snowcat. We need to extract ourselves from this situation and the only way to do that is to get to the snowcat."

She agreed. As much as she didn't want to think about Brayden being out here with dangerous men, every second they were out in the open she felt exposed.

"Which way?" She'd long since lost the direction of the vehicle.

"To tell you the truth, I'm not a hundred percent sure, but I think it's this way." He pointed to their left.

Once more, they started walking. At the edge of the tree coverage a downhill trek waited.

The boots she wore had some traction on the bottoms, but the ice beneath the snow had her slipping and sliding. If it weren't for Axel's grip on her arm, she would have gone down.

"This is dangerous, let's stop." Axel's breathing was labored like hers. "How are you holding up?" he asked when he noticed her clutching her stomach.

Summer was too exhausted to answer. Cramps continued to shoot across her midsection from the endless walking. She couldn't imagine the stress this was putting on the baby.

"Let's rest for a bit." He dusted off a fallen tree for her to sit. Through the limited visible space, every angle looked the same.

"I don't see any other way down," Axel told her after a few moments' rest. "But thankfully we don't have far to go. Are you okay with continuing?"

She wasn't but they didn't have a choice. "I'm okay."

Axel kept his arm through hers as they slowly headed down the mountain. Summer didn't remember the snowcat being this far away. Had they missed it in the storm? "Where is it?"

"I don't see it. It's possible that in the storm we've been going the wrong direction." He glanced around them.

The thought was terrifying. What if they couldn't find it or their way back?

Camo trotted away and was quickly swallowed up in the whiteout.

"He may be on to something." They quickly followed when he barked. An object soon appeared through the snow. It was the snowcat. The dog stood next to it sniffing the tracks.

Axel laughed. "Thank you, Camo." The dog looked up as they approached. "Let's get out of here." Axel opened the door and helped Summer inside. Camo leaped up into the cab, no doubt happy to be out of the weather.

Axel got in and started the machine once more. He didn't waste time heading back up the direction they'd come at a slow and steady pace.

"Who do you think was behind the light we saw?" she asked.

Axel looked her way. "There's no doubt it was one of the people searching for us. They probably found the snowmobile and the three dead men and figured we were behind it."

She wondered about those who had been at Brayden's home. Where had they gone and what had they done with Brayden?

The snowcat continued climbing. "It shouldn't be much farther until we top the mountain," Axel told her. "From there it should be fairly smooth going. We need to reach the sheriff's office."

Those were welcomed words and yet Summer couldn't let herself relax. Ray was coming after her with everything he had. Did he know about the evidence she'd stashed away? If he did, she didn't believe it would matter how much money the baby might fetch—he'd kill Summer to silence her and probably not before he tortured her to find out where she'd hidden the thumb drive.

Something moved in the storm off to her left. She squinted through the windshield, but it was gone. Had she imagined it? Was she seeing bad guys everywhere?

She drew in a breath.

"Everything okay?" Axel asked.

"I'm not sure. I thought I saw something to my right."

Axel glanced past Summer. "Wait, I see something, too." The words barely cleared his lips when gunfire exploded around them. The all-out weapon's attack had him swerving away as shots whizzed off the snowcat. If they lost the machine, they'd be on foot and there was no way of knowing how many people were out there.

They headed away from the shooters. "There's no place you can get that's safe. The cab is all glass," Summer shouted.

And the speed they were capable of going wasn't fast enough to outrun the men. The shots continued to rain all around them.

"I count two shooters," Axel told her while searching

to her right where the men continued firing on them. "Can you drive this thing?" he asked unexpectedly.

The only thing she'd ever driven was a buggy back on the farm. Ray had drivers who moved the girls from place to place.

"It's simple. Here's the gas and the brake. Take the wheel and head away from the shooting. I'm going to try something."

As much as she didn't want him to put his life in more danger, a standoff might be their only option.

Axel opened the door and waited for Summer to take the controls.

He jumped out and slipped toward the back of the machine. She shut the door and kept driving, remembering what he'd told her.

A round of shots coming from behind had her jerking that way. Gun barrel flashes coming from Axel's direction were followed by a distant scream. He'd hit one.

The firing continued. Summer ducked when several of the shots pinged off the glass. Camo growled and leaped into the seat she'd vacated. "No. Camo. Down, boy."

The dog did as she asked.

She glanced back and saw Axel using the cover of the snowcat to protect him from the gunfire that continued. A heartbeat later, another scream confirmed the second shooter was down.

Was that all there was?

Axel appeared beside her and knocked on the glass. She jumped in alarm, but found the brake pedal and pressed down as he opened the door and climbed in. She was glad to give him back the controls.

"I think that was all of them for now." He closed the door and hit the gas pedal. The snowcat started up again.

"Where'd they come from?" She knew Ray had lots of men keeping his organization running. He'd bragged about how he had a virtual army protecting him.

"They're probably the same ones who were at Brayden's place. There could be more."

She had no doubt.

The machine topped the mountain and moved onto level ground. At least that was something.

Getting through the woods with the machine was difficult. The trees grew close together. There was barely room to walk in some places.

Axel maneuvered the vehicle to the right. "Brayden cleared a path especially for the snowcat. We need to find it for easier traveling."

As they moved along, Summer couldn't get what had happened back there out of her head. These men seemed to know the layout of the land well. Something Ray told her once flashed through her mind and she grabbed Axel's arm without thinking.

"What is it?" His attention went to the darkness at her side.

"Ray told me he still has family here that he visits… He'd know the area."

She shivered at the thought.

"Did he ever say where he lived?"

She tried to remember anything useful and couldn't. "No, only that he'd lived here before, oh, and I think he mentioned having a brother."

"Does the brother still live here? I'm wondering if he's using his brother for intel as to what's happening in the area. Where the police are working. Things about the previous case that still aren't settled."

"I don't know." She wouldn't put anything past Ray, including using his own flesh and blood to get what he wanted.

As she glanced out at the darkness pressing in, Summer could almost feel the danger lurking just beyond the safety of the cab...waiting to pounce.

Axel could barely see anything in front of them. Would they be able to find the road leading into town? Normally, the snowcat wouldn't be traveling under these severe conditions. Brayden used it when it was daylight and not in the middle of a blizzard.

In the middle of a storm, it was impossible to see danger until they were right on top of it. If it hadn't been for those men using flashlights and Summer just happening to glance in that direction, they both could be dead.

"Can you think of anything else Ray might have mentioned in the past that could help us?" He knew it was a long shot, but he needed to know.

She leaned back in her seat. "He said a lot of things. Ray loved to hear about himself. He used to brag about how far he'd come from his simple upbringing. He'd make fun of his family as if they were beneath him."

Axel's mouth thinned. "How did he end up in Ohio if he's from around here?"

"When we first met, he told me he was working for a business in town. Of course, that was a lie. I overheard him telling some of his cronies once that he had worked his way up to run the organization. He'd become successful with his bosses in the past by knowing just the right type of girls to pick."

The man's brutality was revolting. "When this is over, I'm going to make it my personal mission to bring him down," he said with enough anger, it had her turning toward him.

She slowly smiled. "Thank you, but I don't want you going down that dark path. I don't want anything bad to happen to you."

The look in her eyes took his breath away. He studied her pretty face for a second longer before staring straight ahead. There was no denying he cared about Summer—how could he not. She'd suffered so much at Ray's hands and yet she was still fighting. He swallowed several times but the lump in his throat wouldn't go away. She put him to shame. Though his faith had grown strong, he'd held on to the anger he felt over losing Erin all these years. He'd blamed God. Himself. The enemy for her death. He'd let it isolate him from most forms of human contact. Brayden was the only close friend he had, and Axel believed it was because they shared what it was like to have seen combat. It was hard to explain that to a civilian.

Summer had her hands clasped over her baby as if protecting it from the dangers outside. Camo was curled up at her feet as if he'd known her forever. She must have felt him watching her, because she turned. Just for a moment, their eyes held. Things he wished he could understand there gave him hope. If their future together was only brief and he was to be there for her and her baby for a short time, it would be enough.

He looked away and pulled out the sat phone once more. Not that he had much hope, but he didn't want to think he'd left anything on the table without trying everything he could to save them.

The sudden static on the line gave him hope. He dialed for help. It rang once and then dropped.

"Almost," he said with frustration. "I'll keep trying." Maybe it was just the location.

Through the darkness, the landscape in front of them became confusing. The trees were getting shorter. Before he put two and two together, he realized they'd reached the edge of cliff on the way down.

"Hold on." He just had time to get out before the snowcat flew off the side of a steep downhill fall.

Summer screamed and closed her eyes.

Axel gripped the wheel tight and braced for a hard hit. He reached for Camo who was hunkered at Summer's feet. The machine struck the ground hard and plowed along for several hundred feet, taking out trees along with it.

Another scream from Summer followed. They were headed for a sheer drop-off.

Lord, please don't let us die here. The prayer tumbled through his head as he fought with everything he had to keep the machine upright.

The brakes seemed not to be in effect as the speed picked up. One of the tracks on the snowcat snapped free, jerking the machine sideways.

"Axel, watch out!" Summer warned.

"I can't control it." He gritted his teeth and stomped on the brakes until he could smell them overheating.

"If we go over it's going to be bad," Axel told her. So many things he wanted to say didn't feel right in the moment.

The snowcat shuddered along as it brought down trees. He stood up and stomped even harder. Axel fearfully watched the trees coming up quickly. Several were huge pine trees. He could no longer steer the machine but if they could hit one of the trees, it might stop their momentum. A large tree appeared in front of them.

"Oh no, oh no, oh no." The words slipped from his lips as he watched the nightmare approaching. He barely got the words out before the snowcat slammed against it at full speed. The sound of metal crunching—glass breaking—was like nothing he'd heard before.

"Cover your eyes with your arm," he managed and closed his eyes to keep shards of glass from damaging them. The impact of the crash seemed to keep going forever. Axel smacked his head on the side of the shattered window and felt the world around him go black.

Axel had no idea how long he'd been out, but he awoke to pain. Everywhere. Coming from his temple. His shoulder. His face stung as if needles were attacking it.

A low moan from close by had his eyes shooting open. Had it come from him or…at his feet, Camo looked up at him. The dog appeared unscathed. "You okay, boy?"

Camo acknowledged his concern with a lick. The dog hadn't been strapped in. Axel couldn't imagine what he'd gone through.

Axel turned his head toward Summer, and another sharp pain followed the movement. He struggled to focus. Her head was against the headrest and turned slightly toward him. She wasn't moving.

"Summer!" He swiftly unbuckled himself and shook her. "Summer, are you hurt?" The baby!

She had a dark smudge in the center of her forehead. No doubt where she'd smacked it against something.

He tried to use his right hand to examine the injury, but the pain was too much. His shoulder had slipped out of joint upon impact.

"Summer, wake up." He shook her again and she moaned, her eyes slowly opening.

She stared at him confused for the longest time. "What happened?"

"We crashed. Can you move? Is anything broken?"

She seemed to be in shock. "I'm not sure." She moved her arms and legs. "I think I'm okay." When she finally was able to focus, she gasped. "Axel, your face. You're bleeding. There's glass embedded everywhere."

He lifted his left hand and felt the debris that had struck him. "The window shattered." He searched for Camo who was still in the floorboard at Summer's feet.

He patted the frightened dog. "Good boy."

The snowcat groaned and shifted dangerously close to the edge. The tree was all that was keeping the machine from rolling over the cliff. Axel had no idea if it would hold for long.

"We have to get out of here," he told her. "The tree could give way at any time." He tried his door. It wasn't moving. "We'll have to try and get out through the other side." They switched seats.

The snowcat's headlights were still on. He could see a little bit and the lights from inside the cab would help. Still, one false move.

He shoved at the other door. It was far worse than the driver's side.

"I'll have to crawl out the front." He had a thought and searched through the contents of the glove box. "A flashlight. Thank you, Brayden." Axel clicked it on and shined it around outside. The pine tree was right up against the Snowcat. He focused the light on the ground. The drop-off was just past the tree, which appeared to be half-uprooted.

At eight months pregnant, there was no way Summer could fit through the opening. He'd have to get the door open and fast.

He didn't want to tell Summer how bad their situation was. Axel picked the few remaining shards of glass free and bent over to make it through the opening while being careful not to make contact with his injured shoulder.

Having to use only his left arm made getting free of the snowcat nearly impossible. He dropped down. The jarring of his body hitting the ground raced through his knees up to the injured arm. He bit back a scream.

"Are you okay?" Summer asked, leaning out of the cab.

It took a second for the pain to ease. "I think so." He once again tried the door, but it wouldn't budge. The snowcat was busted beyond use. "I'm going to try and free the driver's door from outside."

With the flashlight aimed at his feet, Axel worked his way carefully around to the other side.

After several tries, the door still wouldn't release. He tried not to show his concern.

"Wait—I remember Brayden telling me he keeps a toolbox in the snowcat." Axel searched through one of the storage compartments and found nothing. "It must be on the other side." As he headed back around, the machine shifted, sliding further against the tree. The tree gave way a little more. Summer screamed. Time was running out.

He hurried to the storage and found a crowbar. He'd have to pry the door open, and he just hoped there was time.

Axel returned to the driver's side and positioned the crowbar against the lip of the door. It was hard to gain enough leverage with one good arm, but he put his entire weight against the bar and the door opened slightly. The snowcat groaned under the movement.

"Hurry, Axel," she called. "I'm not sure how much longer we have."

He gathered his strength and pried again. The door

screeched, and the snowcat moved again. Finally the door gave way, and he threw it open.

Camo jumped down beside him, waiting for Summer.

The snowcat slipped further. The tree cracked. "It's giving way! There's no more time." Axel reached up and wrapped his arms around Summer, hauling her from the machine. He fell backward and she landed on top of him.

A loud cracking followed as the tree broke and tumbled down the drop-off. The snowcat slid off behind it. Several heartbeats later, a thunderous crash resounded from below.

Their only means of escape was now gone.

Slowly he shifted her from on top of him. "Let's get back to Brayden's and treat our injuries." He felt in his pocket and breathed out a sigh. The sat phone was still there.

Axel rose and helped Summer to her feet using his good arm. It took him a second to recall the direction of the cabin.

Once they started walking, Axel noticed Camo had a limp. His friend was hurting.

"Poor Camo," Summer said when she spotted the dog favoring one side.

"Camo, stop." Axel went over to the dog and felt the injured leg. Camo whimpered. "I'm sorry buddy. It's not broken. I'll need to secure it so there's no further damage, though." He peeled off his jacket. Tearing off a strip of cloth to use was next to impossible. "I can't do anything with this dislocated shoulder."

"Here, let me." Summer took the jacket from him and tore off a large piece of the liner.

"You'll have to wrap it tight," he said and hated feeling useless.

She followed his instructions and secured the dog's injured leg while Camo submitted, realizing she was there to help.

Once she'd tied off the cloth, Axel studied her work. "That's a good job. How'd you learn to bandage like that?"

"From living on a farm and taking care of the animals."

He grinned and clumsily slipped his jacket back on. They started walking again. Camo still limped but the brace seemed to help.

He glanced at her. "I'll need your help with getting my shoulder back in its socket."

"Of course. We'll need to get all the glass out of your face before it gets infected."

He nodded. It stung but his shoulder hurt worse. "How are you feeling?" he asked. "You took quite a knock to your head."

Summer felt around the spot that had begun to swell and winced. "It hurts, but it's not too bad."

As they walked, Axel listened for any sign of more of Ray's men coming but it was impossible to hear anything over the weather.

"Maybe we'll arrive back at Brayden's house and find him there waiting for us." He tossed her a crooked smile, which she returned.

"Wouldn't that be nice."

Axel wasn't holding out much hope. "As soon as I'm patched up, I'll take a stab at fixing the Blazer. We need a way out of here. Heading out on foot in this weather won't be a good idea."

Yet they might not have a choice. They couldn't afford to stay still for long.

Summer stopped. "Look, there are the lights."

Axel focused through the storm in the direction she'd pointed, grateful he'd forgotten to turn off the cabin lights.

As they headed toward the house Axel could feel the effects of everything they'd gone through creeping up on him zapping his strength. They both needed rest. Summer showed clear signs of exhaustion.

They needed to warm up, get something to eat, and to rest—and yet he wasn't sure if they'd have time for any of it.

As they neared, his fear that there might be men inside waiting for them had him wanting to protect Summer. "Stay by the side of the house. Let me go inside and do a quick search."

Once she was out of sight, he opened the door and checked each room, realizing the place was as they'd left it earlier.

Axel went out and brought Summer and Camo inside.

"It's empty. Let's sit for a second." The fire in the woodstove was still burning. He added a few more logs before claiming one of the chairs beside Summer.

"I sure hope we've seen the last of Ray's people for a while. We need time to recoup." He grinned, trying to lighten the moment but failed terribly.

Summer smiled sadly at his efforts. "I'm sorry, Axel."

"Don't be. This is all on Ray." But it did seem as if Ray was taking extreme measures to get Summer back. Was it because of something she knew? He voiced his concerns.

She hesitated for a second. "Ray kept his records all online. He'd have me handle them for him. He had the real names of the girls as well as the ones he'd assigned them. Where he'd taken them from, their ages as well as the names of those in his organization and others that he worked with."

He stilled at the confession. "That could be invaluable to law enforcement."

She nodded. "I thought so. One day when he wasn't looking, I copied all the files onto a thumb drive. I was so afraid he'd catch me, but he didn't. I stuck it into my jeans pocket."

Axel couldn't believe how brave she was. "Do you still have the drive?"

She shook her head. "I was afraid of what Ray would do if he found it. I hid it in the wall of the house before I left."

"You're very courageous, Summer," he said softly.

She shook her head. "I don't feel courageous. Everything scares me."

He searched her face. "It won't always be this way."

Looking at her now, he observed things he hadn't taken notice of before, like how the light caught her blond hair and made it shine. The way her brown eyes seemed to hold flecks of gold in their depths. She had a sprinkle of freckles across her nose. She was beautiful. She needed someone to love her and make her feel that way.

He killed that line of thought immediately. That wasn't him. He didn't have it in him…did he?

Axel cleared his throat. "I'll see if I can find something to treat our wounds." He rose without waiting for her to respond.

In the kitchen he searched cabinets until he found antiseptic and bandages along with tweezers for the glass. He filled a bowl with water and grabbed a couple of towels to clean both their head injuries.

Summer rose as he entered. She looked at him tentatively as if she didn't understand what had just happened between them.

Axel set the supplies on the coffee table. "Do you mind helping me get my shoulder back in place?"

She assured him she didn't. "What do I need to do?"

"First I'm going to lie on the floor on my back." He stretched out on the wood floor and extended his arm, gently bending his elbow so that his palm touched the top of his head.

"Can you support my arm?" he asked through gritted teeth.

She quickly knelt and did as he asked. Axel drew in a couple of breaths before he rotated his hand behind his head and toward his neck.

He closed his eyes and waited for the pain to lessen before continuing.

"What can I do to help?" Summer asked. Axel opened his eyes. "Exactly what you're doing." He gradually moved the hand down toward the nape of his neck and reached toward the opposite shoulder. He felt a pop as the shoulder slid back in place. Followed by immediate relief.

"Did it work?"

He tested his arm. "It did." Axel rose. "I need something to use as a sling." He searched around until he found one of Brayden's old T-shirts. With Summer's help, they fashioned it into a makeshift sling.

"That feels much better," he said in relief.

"Let me get the glass from your face and treat your head wound."

Axel was happy to take a seat. Setting the shoulder back in place had zapped his small pool of energy.

Summer sat across from him and began gently removing each piece of glass with tweezers. "There are so many." Each piece stung as she pulled it free. A worried frown emerged. She looked him in the eye and a jolt of awareness shot through his frame.

Summer leaned closer as she worked. Her blond hair brushed against his skin as she gently worked the glass free. He could smell her shampoo.

He closed his eyes to keep from showing her his reaction to her nearness and imagined a time when the threat around them was gone. What would happen then? Would she eventually return to her home? Move on and find someone to care for her?

She was a beautiful person who had suffered so much at Ray's hands. She likely needed time to heal before she could love anyone. In his own way, Axel understood that. Would he ever be able to let go of the guilt from his past and love again? Right now, it felt about as impossible as surviving Ray.

TEN

Her body ached from the effects of the snowcat accident. She was exhausted down to her soul and her heart rate hadn't settled to normal yet. Summer wasn't sure how much more she could take, but she was more concerned for the baby's welfare. The child had been restless throughout the night.

Please, Lord, protect my child. She couldn't lose her baby.

Summer focused on the final piece of glass lodged in Axel's forehead. "This is the last one." She pulled in a breath and extracted it with unsteady hands.

Axel opened his eyes and looked at her, no doubt seeing her weariness. "Are you okay?"

"I'm fine." She dismissed his concern and held up the tiny piece of glass for him to see.

"Thank you." He started to get up, but she stopped him. "Not so fast. Let me clean the cuts and your head injury."

He sat back down and clenched his hands while she carefully dabbed a wet cloth over the bloody gash on his head.

"Am I hurting you?" Her brow knitted together. She'd been trying to be careful.

His eyes clouded. "No, you aren't hurting me." The rough edges of his voice had her searching his face.

She lowered the hand holding the cloth. There was something about him that made her wish for things that wouldn't be possible. Her gaze snagged on his lips. A whisper of a sigh that originated from somewhere deep inside, where Elizabeth and all her hopes and dreams still lived, bubbled to the surface. That small part of her wondered what it would feel like to be kissed by Axel.

But she wasn't that woman anymore and too many horrible things stood in the way of her ever being Elizabeth again.

She jerked back. They watched each other through the space separating them. All her uncertainties were there for him to see, and she didn't know what to say.

Camo growled menacingly, breaking the spell. The dog started for the door. Axel jumped to his feet, standing in front of her. The door flew open, as snow and wind piled in. A man Summer didn't recognize stepped inside, his frantic gaze searching their faces before he fell to the floor unconscious.

"Brayden!" Axel raced to the unconscious man and turned him over. "He's been shot."

Summer shut the door and knelt beside Axel. "How bad is it?" Blood covered Brayden's jacket. She couldn't imagine what was underneath.

Axel opened the jacket and reeled backward in shock. "It's bad." Brayden's shirt was soaked. "He's been shot in the stomach. We need to stop the bleeding."

Summer rose and got a clean towel from the kitchen and handed it to Axel.

He pressed it against the wound. "Can you get some more gauze from the kitchen? There's a roll I can use to bandage the wound after I pack it." He told her where to look, and Summer rushed to the kitchen to the cabinet and found the items.

When she brought them back, Axel had Brayden's sweatshirt pulled up to expose the gash. He removed the cloth.

Blood seeped out. He moved Brayden slightly to see that there was an exit wound.

Summer handed him the gauze and he packed both wounds as much as he could before wrapping it. Though Brayden remained unconscious, he moaned when Axel was forced to turn him over on his side to get the bandage secured.

"I'm sorry, buddy," he said, his expression grave. Once he'd finished, he tugged the sweatshirt back into place.

"That's a serious injury," he told Summer. "The bandage will hopefully keep it from bleeding too much, but he's lost a lot of blood already." He looked over his shoulder. "He's freezing. I'm going to see if I can move him closer to the fire."

Summer moved the chairs out of the way.

Axel carefully wrapped his arm around Brayden's upper torso and lifted him off the floor. Once more his friend groaned in pain. He moved Brayden to the sofa while Summer found a quilt and placed it over him.

Camo came over to sniff Brayden's hand before settling in front of him.

"What do we do now?" Brayden was in serious condition, and they didn't have any way of calling for help.

Axel brought out the sat phone and tried it again. "It's still not connecting." He rubbed his forehead and checked Brayden's pockets. "He doesn't have his cell phone with him—not that it would be any better than the sat phone. There's only one option I can think of. I'm going to see if I can get the Blazer working. Can you keep watch over Brayden?"

She willingly agreed but she was worried about Axel. "What if Ray's people are close? You could be in danger if you go out there alone." Her worst fear was Brayden had been followed.

"I'll sweep the space around the house to check for any sign of them." He started for the door. "Lock up behind me…just in case."

She hated the possibilities left unsaid. At the door, she decided that Axel's searching gaze was something she would remember for the rest of her life. She wished she had the courage to ask what it meant. Did he feel something like her or was it all in her head?

Without a word, Axel stepped out and closed the door behind him. Summer slid both the dead bolt and the chain lock into place before she turned to look at Axel's friend.

Camo made a noise as she approached. He looked up at her with soulful eyes as if he was worried about Brayden, too.

"I don't know what to do for him, Camo." But she did.

Summer slowly sank to her knees and prayed for Brayden. "Please, *Gott*, don't take his life. Please let him live."

Her eyes opened slowly to find Brayden still unconscious, his head positioned at an awkward angle. Summer went to the bedroom and retrieved a pillow before placing it beneath him.

Brayden groaned in pain, his eyes shooting open. "Who are you?" he whispered in a scratchy voice.

"I'm Summer. I came here with your friend Axel."

He looked around the room. "Where is he?"

"Outside. He's trying to get your SUV working so we can leave."

Brayden's frown deepened as he appeared to be trying to remember what happened.

"Someone disabled both the Blazer and your snowmobile," Summer explained.

He closed his eyes briefly. "I remember. They broke in and came after me, but I managed to get out through the back window. I made it halfway to the county road when they shot me." He stopped and dragged in a couple breaths. "I lost my phone along the way. Wasn't sure I'd make it back. The radio." He struggled to sit up.

Summer rushed to his side. "You mustn't move."

Brayden spotted the radio and fell back against the pillow. "It's busted."

"They wanted to make sure you couldn't call for help," Summer told him.

"It's not safe here." The truth had her stomach in knots. "I did my best to disguise my direction, but I'm pretty sure I left a blood trail. They'll come looking here eventually."

Summer cast a troubled look toward the door. She prayed Axel was able to get the SUV running again before that happened.

"Can I have some water," Brayden croaked. "My throat feels as dry as a desert."

"Of course. I'll get it." Summer went to the kitchen and filled a glass. "Here you go." She held it up to his lips.

Brayden took only a few sips. "Thank you," he murmured, his words slurred.

"You should rest." He didn't respond, but his eyes closed.

Brayden's words played uneasily through her head. *I'm pretty sure I left a blood trail.*

Even in the storm, their pursuers would be able to follow the trail.

She walked to the window and looked out. From the direction of the garage a tiny bit of light shone. "Hurry, Axel."

She checked the locks on the back entrance and returned to Brayden. He appeared to be unconscious again.

As carefully as possible, she checked his wound. So far,

there wasn't any fresh blood on the outside of the bandage. That had to be a good sign.

Too anxious to sit still, Summer paced the room. Camo left his post at Brayden's feet and walked with her. She glanced down at the animal who had won her heart almost from the beginning. "Thank you for keeping me company."

Camo seemed to understand.

On her third trip around the room a noise near the front of the house grabbed her attention. A vehicle. Her first thought was Ray's men had found them.

The vehicle stopped. What did she do? She pulled out the weapon Axel had given her. No matter what, she'd do her best to protect Brayden.

Someone knocked.

Summer froze. The gun shook in her hand. The men hunting them wouldn't be polite enough to knock, surely.

"It's me, Summer." Axel. She quickly unlocked the door and opened it. He rushed inside covered in snow.

The Blazer was parked outside behind him. "You got it running."

"I did. Thankfully, the Blazer is old and uses simple means to run. They loosened the distributor cap. I tightened it and the battery cables. It fired right up." He swung toward Brayden. "How's he doing?"

"Resting." She told him what Brayden had said. Axel's hands balled at his side.

"All the more reason to get out of here before they arrive." He went over and studied his friend. "If those men are near the county road, then we can't go that way. We'll have to take a detour."

He gently shook his friend. It took several tries before Brayden awakened.

"Hey, buddy. How are you feeling?"

Brayden cringed. "Like I've been shot."

Axel laughed. "Well, we're going to get out of here and get you some help. The Blazer is running. Can you stand?"

Brayden tried but fell backward.

"That's okay. I've got you." Axel wrapped his arms around the other man and lifted him to his feet. Brayden swayed unsteadily, his full weight slamming into Axel. Axel staggered but managed to hold his friend.

He waited until Brayden appeared steady before they slowly started for the door.

Summer opened the door and struggled to hold onto it when the wind tried to snatch it from her hands. Camo trotted out into the storm, his head darting around as he sniffed the air for danger.

"I'll get some more gauze and bandages for the road." Once the two men were out, Summer grabbed the supplies along with a quilt and pillow for Brayden then shut the door.

"Let's get you in the back seat where you can lie down," Axel told his friend.

Summer placed the pillow inside. She did her best to help lift Brayden into the seat. He screamed in pain when his injured body hit the seat too hard.

"Sorry, buddy." Axel's face revealed his hurt that his friend was suffering.

Summer placed the quilt over Brayden. "He's going to make it," she assured Axel when he seemed frozen in place staring at his injured friend. "But we have to hurry, Axel." She climbed in beside Brayden and put pressure on the wound.

Axel snapped out of his daze and opened the driver's side door. Camo leaped inside.

He put the Blazer in Drive. "It's too risky going the way of the county road but I don't think the Blazer will make it down the same way we came up." He stared out the windshield and she could tell he was fighting fatigue. Though it was now daylight, the storm was creating havoc on visibility. "We'll have to go back through the woods and then down that way. It's not as steep as the path we came up with the snowcat. Still, I hope the Blazer's up to the trek." He put the vehicle in gear and carefully turned it around.

"I hope Abram and Lainey are safe," Axel said. As they started for the trees ahead, he told her they'd be going close to the Amish community once more. "If those men follow, we'll be bringing even more danger close to the community. Unfortunately, we don't have a choice. Brayden needs a doctor's help."

She could tell he was worried. "It will be okay." She touched her stomach. It had to be. She couldn't go back to Ray.

"The good news is it will take us closer to a paved road just past the community."

"That's something." She forced a smile before looking down at Brayden who appeared to be resting. "He's still sleeping."

"Rest is the best thing for him right now." He glanced back at his friend. "I just hope the trip down isn't too harrowing."

The SUV entered the trees at a crawl. Summer hadn't realized it, but she held a tight grip on her seat. The unknown waiting for them was filled with all sorts of dangerous possibilities.

Axel watched behind them. "So far, I don't see any sign of them. Brayden, how are you holding up?" Nothing but silence.

"Can you check on his wound?"

"He's unconscious. I'll check on his injury." Summer

lifted Brayden's sweatshirt and her heart sank. "It's soaked through."

"We need to change it." He put the SUV in Park and got out removing the sling. Camo started to follow but Axel stopped him.

He got in on the other side of Brayden. Working to change the bandage in such a cramped space was a challenge in itself.

Summer handed him the gauze once he'd removed the soiled bandage.

"Keep an eye out for any movement," he told her. "It makes me nervous to be sitting still for too long."

She searched the darkness around them. So far, there was no sign of the bad men, yet she had no doubt they were still out there searching.

Brayden mumbled in his sleep. Summer couldn't make sense of it. "What's he saying?"

"Something about being betrayed." Axel shook his head. "I'm not sure what he's talking about." He finished bandaging and hastily returned to the driver's seat. In a matter of seconds, they were moving again. "I'm really worried about him. He's lost a lot of blood."

Brayden's struggle filled her with guilt. This was her fault. "Ray won't stop until he has me. He doesn't care how many innocent people he hurts in the process."

The storm showed no sign of letting up. Through the swirling snow outside her window something caught her attention, and she leaned closer to the window. "Axel, I see lights again."

His frantic gaze searched through the storm. A glow appeared. "That's close." He whipped the steering wheel in the opposite direction, turning the Blazer away from the lights. "I'm hoping the storm will keep them from seeing us. We can't afford to not use the headlights after what happened with the snowcat."

Once more the lights disappeared. Summer leaned closer, waiting, but they didn't return. "I don't see them anymore." Her frown deepened. "Where did they go?"

Camo jumped up onto the seat beside Axel, a low growl emanating from him.

"What is it, boy?" Axel's attention was on the dog as Camo stared out the passenger window.

Something moved in the snow. Several men became visible. A flashlight beam reached into the backseat where Summer sat. Flashes followed. A heartbeat later, the crack of gunfire confirmed they were under attack.

Axel jerked the wheel to the left and punched the vehicle as fast as he could. "We can't afford to keep going this way for long. The drop where the snowcat went off is just up ahead."

Brayden moaned again. Summer held on tight as the SUV bounded across the rugged countryside.

"Duck," Axel warned. Summer got down low and prayed they'd be able to escape before one of them was shot—or they reached the drop-off that meant certain death.

Another round of gunfire had Axel flinching as the shots fell short of the Blazer. Thankfully, he was able to stay ahead of the men on foot. "You should be safe to sit up. I'm going to start moving away from the cliff now." He carefully changed direction.

Brayden opened his eyes. "I heard gunshots. What's going on?"

"Glad you're back with us." Axel explained the attack. "We're going to head down and skirt around the Amish community."

Axel glanced at Summer in the rearview mirror. This was her story, and he wouldn't tell it without her permission. She slowly nodded and he did his best to explain.

"I can't believe this is happening again." Brayden slowly sat up clutching the quilt. "I'm so sorry you've had to go through such horrible things, Summer."

A simple nod was all Summer seemed capable of giving.

Brayden broke into a fit of coughing that had him grabbing his stomach. His body went limp, and he slumped down on the seat.

"He's passed out again." Summer checked the wound. "Axel, he's really bleeding badly."

"We need a place to get out of sight, but I can't see anything." Axel searched the wintry haze. Beside him, Camo barked a few times. Axel glanced his way. "What is it, boy?"

The dog continued to bark without looking at Axel. He jerked his head forward. "Oh, no. Hold on, Summer." A huge tree appeared from the swirling snow. He couldn't hit it. They couldn't lose their only means of transportation. He had a severely injured man and a pregnant woman. This couldn't happen.

With only a few seconds to spare, he swerved around the tree. Once they were in the clear, Axel breathed out a huge sigh of relief.

"That was far too close. How is he?" Axel stopped the car.

Summer once more checked the wound. "It's bad. Blood has soaked through the bandages already."

"Do you think you can redo them by yourself?" Axel glanced over and cringed at the amount of blood Brayden had lost. He couldn't let his friend die.

"I think so, but we're almost out of gauze and bandages."

His hands tightened on the wheel and sweat beaded on his forehead as he sat forward, getting as close to the windshield as he could just to see anything more than a few feet in front of them.

"How much farther?" Summer asked, her tone worried. "He really needs a doctor."

He tried to think clearly. How far had they traveled? Axel couldn't remember coming this way except maybe once. What if they were going the wrong way? He forced the voices of doubt down. "Several miles, I think." The answer sounded anything but confident. Summer and Brayden were depending on him, and he had no real knowledge of what they'd be facing as they headed down the mountain.

Lord, please help me. I can't let them down.

Summer touched his shoulder. He met her eyes in the rearview mirror.

"You've got this."

The strength he saw in her made him believe—he had to. He slowly smiled. "Thank you." Axel covered her hand with his.

After losing Erin, Axel couldn't imagine feeling anything for another woman. He couldn't go through that much pain again. Summer made him see he wasn't the only one suffering. She was fighting for her life and her child's while he'd retreated to his mountain hideout to live in isolation. He didn't want to do that anymore. He wanted to live.

"He's resting a bit more comfortably now." She removed her hand and checked Brayden's pulse. "It's steady. That's something."

She was trying to make him feel better, but Axel had seen enough gunshot injuries during combat to know that the one Brayden sustained was critical. If they couldn't get him medical attention soon… As he continued driving, he searched for any familiar sign, yet all he saw was a storm that was frightening. It swallowed up everything in its path and cloaked any would-be landmarks with white.

He reasoned they were still some ways up the mountain.

One bit of hope he held on to: those men wouldn't be able to communicate with their teammates or Ray. A small advantage. With the storm blasting, he didn't believe the gunfight they'd gone through could be heard by anyone not in the immediate area.

It was going to be okay. *They* were okay. He petted Camo's head. The dog seemed to realize his comfort was needed because he licked Axel's hand.

Laughter bubbled up inside him. "Thanks, boy—I needed that." Camo settled down beside him seemingly unconcerned. If the dog wasn't on edge, maybe it was going to be okay.

"No!" Brayden mumbled several times before his eyes shot open and he tried to sit up. Summer did her best to keep him still.

"Don't try to move. You're still bleeding." Axel did his best to help quiet his friend.

"We have to get to the house," Brayden blurted out.

"You mean your home? Brayden, we left your place a while ago…remember?"

Brayden shook his head and then winced and grabbed his side. "I'm not talking about my place. My old homestead."

Brayden had told him about his family's old place many times. Both of his parents had died within months of each other, and the house had sat vacant for years. When Axel had questioned his friend about his parents' deaths, Brayden said his father had died when his vehicle had gone over the side of the mountain. His mother died a few months later from what was believed to be an undetected heart condition. Axel had always thought it strange they'd died so close together, but he'd heard of cases where one spouse died and the other passed away a short time later supposedly from a broken heart.

"I think he's up to something bad." Brayden slurred his words, his eyes glazed.

"Who?" Axel was totally confused. He took his attention off the stretch of land he could see through the headlights to glance at Brayden.

"He's passed out again." Summer checked Brayden's pulse. "Do you have any idea what he meant?"

Axel shook his head. "No. He could be talking about something he witnessed in battle. Brayden told me he still has nightmares from that time."

"I can't imagine what you both have gone through," Summer said softly.

She was concerned for him. After everything she'd endured, Summer worried about *him*. His heart filled with feelings he didn't know how to deal with. He cared about her. Couldn't bear the thought of Ray winning after all he'd done to her.

"Axel… I'm." She hesitated, and he believed she was going to apologize.

He shook his head. "You've done nothing wrong, Summer. There's nothing to apologize for. You're the victim."

She flinched and he realized he'd said the wrong thing.

"I hate that word." She scraped her hair back from her face. "Even though I am a victim, I don't want to feel like one." She touched her belly. "This little one needs me not to be a victim."

"You've gone through something awful, but it's made you strong—maybe stronger than you ever thought possible."

She didn't look away and his heart responded eagerly to the hope in her eyes.

"I didn't think he would do this. I didn't," Brayden rambled deliriously, and Summer's attention shifted to him. She tucked the blanket around him, which would hopefully help keep him still.

"I haven't seen any sign of Brayden's abandoned house, have you?" she asked.

"No, but even if there was a place, we can't stop. We've got to get Brayden to the hospital in Elk Ridge."

She nodded and stared out the window. She possessed a beauty that would only grow with time. She had the glow of a pregnant woman, but there was a fighting spirit in her that shone through, too. She would protect her child to the death. And he would protect her because he couldn't lose her. Couldn't lose the woman who had made him feel like a human again.

Going through this ordeal with Summer had reminded him of how good it felt to help someone else. And it had made him realize he'd missed having that special human connection in his life like he'd had before. Sure, he had Brayden and some other friends, but he missed what he and Erin had shared. Missed being attracted to someone. Falling in love.

His and Summer's almost kiss popped into his head. An unexpected tender moment that proved he was still capable of feeling something.

"Axel." The panic in her voice grabbed his attention.

He followed where she pointed. "I don't see anything."

She leaned closer to the window. "I thought I saw a light."

Axel braked and searched through the storm. "There is something. A single light." Was it the Amish community?

He didn't believe so. Their homes were lit by lanterns. That light appeared much brighter than what would be put out from a lantern. Had they veered off course and were now heading away from the community? He shared his fears with her. "Not that it matters. If that doesn't belong to a flashlight, then chances are we're somewhere close to a farm."

The relief on her face was intense. "Maybe they'll have a landline."

"It's possible." Though he didn't say as much, he didn't want to dash her hopes. Most people nowadays didn't really have landlines. Still, some of the old timers stubbornly kept them and Axel was certain they'd come in handy when cell service wasn't available.

"Let's head toward the light." It didn't look so far away. Still, with the storm distorting everything, it could be on the other side of the drop-off. He'd have to be careful. One false move could end in their deaths.

Axel eased along at a crawl. After they'd gone some ways, he stopped.

"Do you see something?" she asked.

"No, but I'm worried I won't see the slope until it's too late." He faced her. "I'm going to get out and walk a little way down."

She studied him, as if looking for something he wasn't telling her.

"I'll be back soon." He got out and closed the door. Axel searched the darkness with a sense of unease slithering down his spine. Where had the shooters from earlier gone? Unless they'd gotten turned around in the storm, he had no doubt they'd keep coming.

He'd taken only a few steps when the confusion of the

whiteout set in. Was he heading in the right direction? He turned toward the SUV, the lights barely visible.

Axel drew in a breath and applied reason to the problem. He'd been heading for the mysterious light, so the Blazer would be pointed toward it, which meant the direction he was going should be safe.

Because what had happened so far wouldn't let him relax, Axel retrieved his handgun and checked the clip. Almost empty. He switched out the clip for a full one. As he started walking again, Brayden's strange ramblings niggled at his mind. Was his friend reliving his battle days? Delirium had a way of making even the strongest confused at times. Axel had certainly seen it enough during the war.

He kept going for a while and turned. The headlights were still visible. They would lead him back to Summer and Brayden. He was okay. He peered deep into the winter onslaught. Where had the light gone? It had been there a few minutes earlier.

He panned out farther, but the light was gone. Axel didn't believe Ray's men could've regrouped so quickly after the last attack with no likely form of communication. Was the flashlight coming from one of the Amish farms? Most of the morning chores on the farms would be done by now. It could be someone working…

An uneasy feeling had him swinging toward the Blazer. It seemed miles away as Axel started running for it.

Crack! The alarming sound had him ducking low. Gunfire. A shot flew past his right side. Axel raced toward the Blazer's headlights.

Shots continued to fly around him followed by another shocking sight. More lights closing in from the opposite side. They'd almost reached the Blazer. His heart exploded against his chest. As he neared the SUV, he yelled for Summer to get down.

Axel opened fire over the top of the vehicle to force the attackers back.

Grabbing the door handle, he yanked it open. Inside, Camo was on the passenger floorboard.

"Are you hurt?" he asked Summer, who was crouching behind the driver's seat. Without wasting time, Axel jerked the vehicle into Drive and floored the gas.

"I'm okay," she said, clearly shaken. "They came out of nowhere."

His full attention was on keeping the SUV from crashing into a tree as they sped down the mountain while taking heavy gunfire. The back window shattered and Summer screamed. Axel ducked low amidst the rampage. Another round hit the back tire, blowing it immediately. He struggled to keep the vehicle from flipping.

The shooters continued firing relentlessly. Several emerged from the snowy world to Axel's right and destroyed the driver's side window, almost hitting Axel. He swerved and ducked and did his best to keep going.

"Axel!" Summer yelled his name over the noise.

"I'm okay." But they had to get away from the shooters because when the next shot came, none of them would survive.

ELEVEN

Summer covered her ears as bullets continued to bounce off the SUV. Brayden moaned, his panicked eyes homing in on hers.

"Stay down," she told him and gently placed her hand against his shoulder. "You can't sit up. It's too dangerous."

"Where's Axel?"

"I'm right here, buddy. Do as Summer says." Axel explained what was happening.

Brayden's eyes closed. For a minute, Summer thought he'd passed out again. "He's bad. He's just bad," he murmured.

"We're losing them," Axel said over the noise. The shots were no longer hitting their mark.

With the back window gone, cold air and snow blew in, immediately dropping the temperature to below freezing. Summer's breath fogged the air in front of her.

Soon, the firing stopped.

"You should be safe to sit up," Axel said from up front. "We're out of range and they've realized it."

Summer slipped into the seat next to Brayden's feet while the Blazer suddenly sputtered and lurched. "What's going on?"

Axel stared at the gauges. "I think the engine was hit. We're losing oil pressure." The vehicle sputtered again.

"Can we keep going like this?" Summer glanced behind. Though some distance behind, flashlights were coming after them.

"I'm not sure how long. Let's hope we can make it down the mountain and to the Amish community where we can hopefully borrow a buggy and get Brayden to Elk Ridge."

Summer caught his worried expression in the mirror.

The tension in the cab built. More sputtering followed as the engine struggled to keep going.

"We're slowing down," Axel groaned. "This isn't good." The vehicle had noticeably lost speed.

"What do we do?" She leaned forward and looked over his shoulder. The oil light was on.

"I'm going to put it in Neutral. We can coast for a while."

"But not forever." She said what he didn't.

"No, not forever." His attention momentarily reverted to Brayden. "At some point we'll be on foot with an injured man."

Summer's heart sank. She understood what that meant. It would be next to impossible to stay out of sight under those circumstances. And almost impossible to keep going in this storm.

She sat back against the seat and looked at Brayden. So many people had been hurt, all because she'd tried to escape Ray's hold. She fought back tears. "Brayden could die."

"I'm not going to let that happen." Axel's voice was steady. "Brayden's strong. We can't lose hope."

She wanted to believe him. Summer brushed her fingers over her eyes. Crying wasn't going to help anything.

Someone touched her hand. She glanced over and noticed Brayden was awake. He must have seen her tears. She tremulously smiled down at him.

"Where are we?" Brayden croaked, shifting his attention to Axel.

"I'm not sure, but we're in trouble." Axel didn't mince words. "The only thing keeping us going now is the downhill momentum of the vehicle."

Brayden slowly attempted to sit up.

"No, you mustn't." Summer braced her hand against his chest.

"It's okay," Axel told her. "We need his help."

She understood. Without Brayden's assistance, they may not survive. She put her arm around his shoulders and eased him into a sitting position.

Brayden closed his eyes for a second as if trying to regain his strength before looking at their surroundings. "It's hard to tell in these conditions, but I believe we're close to my old farm." He stopped for a couple of breaths. "My dad's old truck is still parked in the garage. It ran the last time I was here."

Hope rose inside her until she got a good look at Axel's face. The probability of that happening was next to impossible.

Still, she needed something to hold on to. Keeping the fear at bay was hard. She could see Ray's smug expression and imagined how pleased he would be when he caught her. The things he'd do to her before he killed her.

"Hey, it's going to be okay," Axel whispered. "We're not done fighting yet." He watched her in the mirror, seeing all her fears.

She so wanted to believe him.

The vehicle hit a somewhat level space and slowed even more. She glanced out the window at the nightmare storm and dreaded what lay ahead.

The vehicle rolled to a painstakingly slow stop before the engine coughed several times and died.

Axel tried to start the Blazer again, but it was useless. The damage was too great. "Looks like this is it," he murmured. He turned to where Brayden leaned back against the seat. "Can you give me some idea which way we should head?"

Brayden squinted through the snow falling out the side window. "To your left. I'm almost positive about it."

Almost. Would it be good enough to save them? If they got lost in the storm, Ray's people finding them would be the least of their worries.

"Okay, I'll come around and help you out." Axel forced the door open against the wind and jumped down. Camo was right on his heels.

Summer lumbered from the vehicle. The wind hit her immediately and she almost lost her balance.

"I've got you." Axel materialized close to her. "Hang on to me."

She looped her arm through his. Where she'd once abhorred being touched by anyone, the trust she had in Axel was slowly releasing the power it had over her. *He* wasn't Ray. *He* would never hurt her.

Together, they started around the back of the SUV as fast as the deep snow accumulation would allow.

Once they reached Brayden's side, Axel opened the door. "I'm going to let you go, but I'm right there if you need me."

Summer grabbed hold of the open door as the brutal wind continued to torment her.

Getting the injured man from the back seat took some time. The simple act of getting out of the vehicle left Brayden noticeably struggling for breath. While Axel secured his friend's coat against the weather, Summer caught a glimpse of the bandage. Blood had seeped through the packing and covered the outer dressing. She looked away. Brayden's life was in danger. She couldn't let him die. No matter what, she couldn't let him die because of her.

"We'll take it slow," Axel assured Brayden, who leaned heavily on him. "You're certain it's this way to the house?"

Brayden managed a nod.

With Axel's arm around Brayden's upper chest, they started away from the vehicle. Summer closed the door and stayed close to Axel. Camo quickly took the lead and trotted out in front of them. They'd barely covered any space when Brayden's body went limp.

"He's unconscious again." Axel struggled to hold him up.

"Let me help you." Summer went around to the opposite side of Brayden and positioned her arm just below Axel's.

Walking with an unconscious man between them was difficult enough without the weather playing its part. Cold drilled down through her jacket, past her clothes and chilled her skin after only a brief time of being exposed.

Sweat beaded on her brow. Summer stumbled trying to hold up her share of Brayden's weight.

"Let's take a break." Axel must've sensed her struggle and found a tree to support Brayden.

She didn't have the energy to form a verbal answer. She dragged in a handful of breaths and her body slowly regained strength. Summer watched as Camo inspected the frozen ground around them for scents and eventually gave up.

"It's the weather," Axel said, drawing her attention to him. He nodded toward Camo. "The cold makes it difficult for dogs to pick up scents."

She nodded. "I don't see any lights yet. That's a good thing."

He reached for her hand, and she didn't want to pull free. She wanted to stay here with him—even in the middle of this storm—and let the ugliness that Ray had instilled in her heart heal.

"Yes, it's a good thing." He held her gaze. "Summer…"

She couldn't look away. Summer hung on his every word.

"When this is over, I want to do whatever I can to help you heal." There was something new in his voice. Something like…pity?

Her heart plummeted. He felt sorry for her. She wasn't sure what was worse. That she'd let herself imagine things that weren't there or his pity.

She dropped her gaze to Camo, who had returned to them. "I'll be okay. I just want this over. Once and for all I want to be free of Ray."

He tugged at her hand. "Summer, look at me."

She couldn't. Not with her heart so fragile.

"Oh…no." The drastic change in Axel's tone grabbed her attention right away. The tender moment had passed. He pointed. "Lights. More than one."

Summer swung toward them. Several flashlight beams pierced through the blizzard, which meant they had to be close for them to be able to pick up the lights through the weather.

"We need to get moving if we're going to stay in front of them enough to give us breathing room and hopefully get the vehicle running."

She appreciated him for trying to make her believe that might be possible.

Summer placed her arm around Brayden. With Axel taking on most of the weight, they were mobile again. Each step became a struggle as they moved into the teeth of the wind. She glanced behind. Had the lights gained on them?

"Remember, they're struggling just like we are," Axel said, no doubt to make her feel better. But they had an injured man with them.

Camo sniffed around the ground as if he had hopes of picking up a valuable scent.

Axel suddenly stopped, the instant lack of movement almost pulled her to the ground.

"What is it?" she asked, her attention on his troubled face.

He indicated the ground. "Those are footprints. The snow has partially covered them up. Someone's been this way recently."

"The men behind us maybe?" She glanced over her shoulder again.

"Possibly. If they came this way already, then maybe they won't return if they've cleared the house. Unless they lose their way in the storm."

She and Axel did their best to pick up the pace.

"Do you think Ray knows you have the information from his computer?"

Axel's question jarred her from her weariness. "I'm not sure. I was careful to not draw attention to myself and he never questioned me."

"Still, he knows you have a lot of knowledge about his operation in your head. He's worried enough about what will happen to him if Vitaliy gets wind of his mistake. You know enough to bring down the entire organization and possibly even Vitaliy's part in it. He has to find you."

Axel's words settled uneasily around her. "There's something else."

Summer shuddered as she recounted how Ray had told her he'd killed some people in the past.

Axel swung his head her way. "You mean more than the girls he alleged to have murdered."

She nodded. "It sounded like it happened before he became involved in all of this… Oh." An unexpected cramp shot through her midsection stopping her in her tracks.

Axel pointed to a nearby tree. "We need to take a break." He slowly lowered Brayden to the ground and leaned him against a tree. "I don't see the lights anymore."

She searched the way they'd come. Nothing but the storm biting at their heels. *Please let them get confused by the storm and not follow us.*

"Like how many people?" Axel asked.

The conversation she'd had with Ray years ago was as clear as the day it happened. "He didn't say. I asked him what he was talking about," she said softly, recalling Ray's reaction to the question. "He seemed genuinely shaken that he'd given too much away, and nothing ever frightened Ray." Axel kept his attention on her face as she told him word for word the conversation. "It happened not too long after I'd been taken. Ray would get in these ugly moods." She recalled the darkness that seemed to permeate every part of Ray when this happened. "He'd go from cruel to terrifying like flipping a switch. Anyway, I'd said something that set him off and he grabbed me by the throat." She touched the spot without realizing it. "I thought he would kill me right then." She forced down the fear that was there when she recalled the talk. "He saw the fear on my face, and he laughed." Summer glanced Axel's way. "He actually laughed as if it were funny. Ray told me I'd better watch what I said, or I'd end up like the others he'd killed. This was before he told me about the girls."

"Why do you think the people he spoke about killing back then were different?"

"He seemed to hint that the murders had happened when he was very young. At the last house I was at before I escaped, I remember Ray kept staring out at the barn. I asked him why, and he said that was where it had happened. He forced me to go inside the barn with him and he'd grin with this maniacal expression on his face. He said they were buried right where they needed to be and then he glanced down at the ground." She'd been so scared.

Axel's hands balled at his sides. "You'll need to tell this to the sheriff when we get through this. He'll want to retrieve the thumb drive as well. We want to make sure Ray and his crew don't ever walk out of prison again." He glanced at Brayden, who was now awake. "Hey, how are you feeling?" Axel knelt beside his friend.

Brayden sighed. "Like I'm only slowing you down."

"Nonsense. Let me get you to your feet."

"You should leave me," Brayden croaked out. "It will be faster for you two to go ahead without me."

"I'm not leaving you and that's final." Axel lifted Brayden to his feet. The man swayed unsteadily. "We'll get to the house, and you can rest while I work on the truck."

Summer could tell that Brayden didn't believe it. Yet the man answered, "All right, but I can walk on my own for now."

Axel and Summer flanked him on both sides as they started off. Even Camo appeared to be feeling the weight of the weather. Though still out in front, he wasn't full of energy like before because of the injured leg.

Several times, Brayden stumbled, and Axel caught him.

"Let me help you for a while." Axel placed his arm around his friend. Brayden didn't seem to have the energy to argue.

As they continued downhill, the trees appeared to thin.

"What happened to the forest here?" Summer asked. Just a short time earlier they'd been in thick woods.

"They've been cleared away," Axel answered. "We must be getting close to the house."

Thank You, Gott.

"Look." Axel pointed to a broken-down fence.

"This is the beginning of the old homestead," Brayden murmured, the exhaustion of the trip showing in his barely audible words. "We're close."

Summer wouldn't let herself think about what an impossibility it would be to get the vehicle running after so many years of disuse. At least they had a place to get out of the weather for a bit and hopefully reach the sheriff.

"Brayden, can you get through the fence on your own?" Axel asked.

Brayden pulled in several shaky breaths. "I think so."

"Good. I'll go before you and help you through." Axel ducked down and slipped between two pieces of smooth wire. Camo slipped under as if it were nothing and trotted through the snow sniffing the air.

Axel lifted the top wire with his hands and put his boot against the bottom wire to give Brayden room to ease through.

As soon as Brayden was through, he stumbled and hit the ground. Axel grabbed for him and helped him up.

"Okay?" He waited for Brayden to respond.

Once Brayden was steady on his feet, he held the wires for Summer. The weight of her pregnancy made it difficult to lower herself enough to get through. The top wire scraped her back as she cleared it. She straightened too quickly and the world around her spun. She closed her eyes and willed the familiar dizziness away.

Axel reached her side quickly. "Are you in pain?" She

slowly opened her eyes and looked into his. The concern there warmed her heart. She'd stopped believing in human kindness after what Ray did to her, but Axel stirred up feelings of trust again. Not all men were like Ray. Axel certainly wasn't.

"I'm okay. I stood up too quickly."

He nodded. "Can you keep going?"

"Yes. I'm fine now."

He searched her face, clearly not convinced, but at this point they had no choice. "Stay close to me and if you need a break let me know. I want to make sure you and the baby are safe."

She kept in step beside him as he helped Brayden along the way. As hard as it was for her, she couldn't imagine how Brayden was struggling. "Do you see the house yet?"

Axel focused ahead. "Nothing. But in this storm, it would be impossible until we were almost right on top of it."

He was trying to make her feel better. She smiled over at him and whispered, "Thank you."

He smiled back. "We're close."

"It's up there," Brayden muttered, his words slurred. "I know it's up there." He lifted his hand and pointed straight ahead.

"You sure?" Axel asked because like her, nothing but darkness and the storm could be seen.

Brayden nodded. "I'm sure."

"That's good enough for me," Axel told his friend. They headed in the direction he indicated.

Soon, shapes appeared through the dense snowfall.

"There's the house." Summer couldn't ever remember seeing such a wonderful sight before.

Axel stopped suddenly.

"What is it?" she asked and wasn't sure she could take too many more bad breaks.

"Those footprints from earlier. I have no doubt Ray's men were down this way at some point. What if they left men behind?"

The thought hadn't occurred to Summer.

He watched the house with a frown. "There's a shed over to the left. I need you and Brayden to wait for me inside. I'll clear the house and garage and come back for you."

As bad as she didn't want him to leave her for a second, she understood the importance of making sure they weren't walking into an attack, and Axel was a former soldier. He'd know how to protect himself.

"Okay," she agreed, grateful for his military background. It had saved their lives.

"You both should be able to get inside the shed and out of the weather," Axel said. "I'll leave Camo to help you keep watch."

The dog's ears perked up at the mention of his name.

They reached the small shed and Axel pried the door open. There was an old riding lawn mower inside that didn't look as if it had run in a while. He helped Brayden over to the lawnmower and eased him down onto the seat. "Rest for a bit."

Brayden didn't respond but held his injured midsection, his breathing labored. Summer glanced around the small space. There were a few tools hanging on the wall. A small workbench that ran along the back wall.

"It's considerably warmer here and it's dry." He was trying to put a good spin on things. "At least that's something."

She would stay positive as well. "Yes, it is." Summer walked with him to the door.

"I'll be back as soon as I can." He touched her face and she didn't back away. How could she? She trusted him. There were so many things in his eyes that she'd give anything to understand. "Stay safe. Protect him." He indicated Brayden.

"I will. Take care of yourself, Axel."

He dropped his hand and slowly nodded. Axel glanced down at the waiting dog. "I'm afraid you have to stay, Camo." The dog's disappointment was clear.

Axel opened the door enough to leave. Their eyes connected briefly before he left, and it felt as if her rock had slipped away.

"It's okay, Camo." Summer stroked the dog's head for comfort. Camo eventually accepted his fate and went to explore their surroundings while Summer felt her way to Brayden's side. "How are you feeling?" She could hear his labored breaths. Having to trek through the storm had depleted what little strength he had left.

"I've been better, but I'm hanging in there."

"As soon as we're in the house, we need to examine your wound. The bandage will need to be changed."

He still held his stomach. His hand had to be covered with his own blood. Summer was so afraid they wouldn't be able to get him the help he needed in time.

The door to the shed opened. She swung toward it relieved when Axel appeared.

Camo bounded over to him as if it had been days and not minutes since he'd last seen his master.

"The place is empty," Axel said. "There's no sign anyone's been this way in a while" He came over to the lawnmower, eyeing his friend. "Let's get you inside."

"I can stand," Brayden told him, and Axel stepped back and waited while the other man gripped the steering wheel of the lawnmower and slowly pushed himself up to a standing position. "Lead the way, brother."

Axel kept close to Brayden as he eased to the door.

"I've got it," Axel told him and held it while Brayden and Summer stepped out into the storm. "It's this way." He pointed straight ahead. Camo ran past them, following Axel's quickly disappearing tracks.

They'd taken only a few steps when the storm swallowed up the shed from sight.

Even though the short reprieve from the frigid temperature had helped, the minimal warmth the shed afforded soon disappeared and cold ate through her jacket and clothes once again. Summer couldn't feel her feet. She staggered and Axel caught her arm.

"We're almost there," he said close to her ear. Those words sounded beautiful and yet reaching the house was only the beginning. They still had to get the vehicle running. Get out of here alive…

Stop it.

She did her best to silence the voices of doubt inside that told her she would never escape Ray no matter how much help she had.

"There!" Axel pointed in front of them. The house appeared through the white. As they neared, she noted there was nothing about its state of decay that was comforting.

Camo bounded toward the structure and up onto the porch while everyone else followed much more slowly. Axel assisted Brayden up the steps while Summer clung heavily to the railing.

Once they reached the door, Axel pushed it open, and they went inside.

The temperature was several degrees warmer, and she noticed that Axel had started a fire in the fireplace.

"Thank you." Summer glanced down at her baby. She was so worried. Would her freedom come at the cost of losing her child?

No! She wouldn't believe that. *Gott* hadn't brought them this far only to lose her child.

"I figured we all could use a little fire to warm up." He pointed to the two chairs in front of the fire. "Sit. Both of you."

Brayden sank down onto one of the dusty chairs and closed his eyes, his breathing still labored.

Summer swung to Axel. "We need to change his bandage before it gets infected."

He nodded. "Let me see if I can find something here."

He disappeared into the kitchen while Summer glanced around the dark room lit only by the fire's glow. She wondered about Brayden's past, his family. Axel had said Brayden's parents died.

"This should work." Axel returned carrying what appeared to be a dish towel. "We'll have to reuse the outer bandage but..."

She understood what he meant. It would have to do.

Summer helped him remove first the outer bandage and then the soiled cloth. The gunshot wound was still bleeding. She could tell from the troubled expression on Axel's face that he was worried.

"It should hold for a while." The bleakness in his eyes when he faced her told a different story. Brayden was fading fast.

"I'm going to check out the truck." Axel straightened. As much as he wished there were food and water to strengthen them, the house hadn't been occupied in years. "When I was in the garage earlier I found a few spare parts. Hopefully, it will be enough to get it running. Can you watch out for Brayden? If he gets worse, come find me." Axel did his best to keep his misgivings from Summer but from the despair on her face he believed she knew how bad things were.

She walked him to the door.

"Do you still have the weapon I gave you earlier?"

"I do." She showed it to him.

"Good. Keep it close. I'll try to hurry. Camo can stay with you. If you hear anything suspicious, get out of sight. If you have to fire, shoot to kill."

She nodded hesitantly. "Be careful, Axel." Her beautiful eyes held his. The depth of caring he saw for him there broke his heart. For the first time in a long time, he had something worth living for and it might all be taken from him.

There were many things he wanted to say but how could he when the worst possible scenario was facing them. Instead, he leaned over and kissed her cheek before slipping from the house.

The door closed quietly behind him. His heart felt as heavy as the exhaustion weighing down his legs.

Axel worked his way to the garage and the truck that was in bad shape from what he could tell. But it was their last hope, and he couldn't let Summer and Brayden down.

He shut the door against the cold and went over to the truck that looked far older than the twenty years Brayden said had passed since his dad's death.

Opening the driver's door, he noticed the keys hung from the ignition. Not a good sign. That it had been left untouched for years without being stolen meant it probably wasn't running. Axel tried to crank the engine. The battery made a chugging sound but wouldn't turn over. He stopped, not wanting to drain what little life was left in the battery if the main problem lay somewhere else.

He stepped over to the hood and lifted it. It looked as if

a community of mice had taken up residence. Who knew what kind of wires had been chewed through.

Using the flashlight, Axel cleaned the nests away and searched the motor. He checked the cables to the battery. One had come loose. After tightening it, he looked around for any other culprits. The radiator still had antifreeze in it, which was shocking. What about fuel?

Axel searched around and found a half-full gas can and poured it into the vehicle. After trying everything in his expertise, he got in and tried the key once more. This time, the chugging sounded more promising. Axel stopped for a second, his hands shaking. So much was riding on him getting the truck to run.

"Please, God, they're going to kill us and I'm all out of options. Let this thing start."

He pulled in several unsteady breaths and tried again. The engine turned over. The vehicle sputtered several times before running smoothly.

"Thank You." He looked toward the heavens with gratitude.

Axel got out and opened the double doors, preparing to drive to the house, when a disturbing sight amped up the urgency. Flashlights coming from the opposite way he, Brayden and Summer had hiked in. No doubt these were Ray's men.

He hurried back to the truck and drove from the garage without the headlights. Best not to alert their pursuers to their location. He quickly closed the garage doors, hoping if they did come this way after he, Brayden and Summer were gone, all traces of them would have disappeared.

Axel was worried about his friend. The man was fading fast. This was their only hope at getting Brayden the help he needed and escaping the traffickers. They appeared to be coming at them only on foot at this point, but he believed they had to have some type of transportation that would allow them to move the men from the mountaintop.

"Keep us hidden and keep them on foot." Because there was no way they could outrun the enemy should they be waiting near the Amish community with vehicles.

He pushed the negative thoughts aside. They had transportation. At some point he hoped the sat phone would pick up service. They were safe for now.

Pulling the truck up as close to the house as he could, Axel got out, his attention on the lights. They'd covered a whole lot of territory in a short amount of time. He and Summer wouldn't have long to get Brayden out of the house and get away.

He had no idea how much gas the vehicle had. There hadn't been much in the can. Hopefully they'd have enough to reach Elk Ridge.

He knocked on the door. "Summer, it's me," he said as quietly as possible. She opened the door with the weapon in her hand.

He explained about the flashlights. "They'll reach the house soon. We should leave now."

The fear on her face doubled.

"There's a blanket in the back bedroom. Can you grab it? I'm not sure if the heater works or not and it will keep you and Brayden comfortable." The single cab truck would be a tight squeeze for them all including Camo, but it ran, and they were close to getting away from this nightmare.

While Summer searched for the blanket, Axel went over to Brayden. "I got the truck running. We can get you to the hospital now." Axel wrapped his arm around Brayden's upper body and helped him to his feet. The stress of being shot and on the run was taking its toll. Brayden was no longer lucid and could barely stand on his own.

"Here it is." Summer returned with the dusty blanket.

"It's because of Daddy," Brayden mumbled.

Axel shot Summer a confused look. "Try not to talk, buddy. We're going to get you to the truck." Axel had no idea what demons haunted Brayden but right now he was worried for his friend's life.

Without warning, Camo suddenly bounded to his feet and charged for the front door barking loudly. Axel's worst fear became reality. They were too late.

"It's Ray. He's found us." Summer's terror was evident in her tone.

Axel returned Brayden to his seat and hurried to the window. Several sets of headlights were right outside. Where had they come from? More armed men were at the truck. There would be no escaping in it. If they stayed, they'd die. Like it or not, they were back on foot again.

Axel once more assisted Brayden to his feet. "If we can reach the shed… It's our only hope." But then what? Axel had no doubt their hunters would search every building on the place once they didn't find them in the house. But Axel was all out of ideas, and they couldn't stay here.

With Brayden close, he moved to the back entrance and looked out. "I don't see anything." Still, in the storm and at night, Ray's people could be right on top of them without them realizing it.

"Stay close to me," he said to Summer. Walking out onto the back porch took more courage than he imagined. So far, there was no sign anyone was around here.

He stepped from the veranda. Brayden groaned. Summer stayed so close Axel could feel all her fear. Camo's hackles were raised as they trudged toward the shed.

Up ahead he saw its silhouette.

As they got closer, armed men emerged from all around and came after them.

"Hurry, go back to the house!" Axel yelled as the men started shooting. He all but dragged Brayden back to the house and up the steps. Once inside, he slammed the door closed and locked it. Once he had Brayden seated by the fire, Axel shoved the kitchen table against the back door and searched for something heavy to block the front door. He reached for the sofa.

"Let me help you," Summer said.

He shook his head. She was barely hanging on. "I've got it." It took much of his waning strength to shove the sofa against the door, knowing it would only provide a little deterrent to those determined men.

With a prayer racing through his head, Axel tried the sat phone and caught a signal. His legs felt weak with elation. He didn't wait for the dispatcher to finish speaking. "This is Axel Sterling. We're under attack from armed men near the Amish community at the abandoned farm north of there. We need immediate help." Before the dispatcher could confirm, the call dropped. Axel tried it again, but the signal was lost. Would help come in time?

He rushed to the front of the house. The men were on the porch now. He pushed whatever other furniture he could against the entrance as a barrier that wouldn't hold should they force the door.

Several rounds of fire pelted the house lodging bullets in opposing walls.

"Get down!" Axel yelled to Summer.

She dropped to the floor and covered her head while he dove to shield Brayden.

When the silence returned, Axel tried the phone again. Same results.

God, please, not like this. Not when I promised to help Summer escape these men.

"You're surrounded!" someone yelled. "There's no way out. Come out now. Don't make us have to come in after you, Summer."

Summer.

Axel jerked toward her. She had gone as pale as a sheet.

"That's Ray," Summer said in a shocked voice. "You've got thirty seconds, Summer," her tormentor continued. "Otherwise, I'm coming in after you and you know what I'll do to you and him if you make me come after you."

Summer slowly rose. The defeat on her face was hard to witness. "He's right—he'll kill you." She moved to Axel's side. "He wants me. If I turn myself over to him perhaps Ray will let you and Brayden—"

"That's not going to happen." Axel wasn't about to let her sacrifice herself for him. "I'll die first."

"No." Her face screwed up in pain and she reached up and touched his cheek. "I don't want that. I can't..."

He covered her hand with his and looked into her eyes. "Let me fight for you, Summer. You deserve someone who will fight for you."

A sob escaped.

"I guess we're doing it the hard way," Ray called out.

Something heavy slammed against the door.

"Get out of sight." Axel wrapped her in his embrace and tugged her into one of the bedrooms. "Stay here and get in the closet. I'm going for Brayden."

There was just enough time to haul Brayden into the bedroom and lay him on the bed before the front door gave way followed by the back door.

Axel fired on the advancing men. Camo charged toward one who was almost right on top of Axel.

The perp whirled toward the dog and fired. Camo yelped as the bullet struck his hind leg. The battle-weary soldier didn't give up his mission. He charged the man.

"No, Camo!" Axel couldn't bear the thought of losing his friend. Camo ignored Axel's command. The dog would fight to the death to save Axel.

Axel dove behind the sofa and picked off each person who came into his line of sight, but there were too many. It was a losing battle.

Click, click, click. The sound was one of the most gut-wrenching of all. He was all out of bullets. Falling back on his training, Axel grabbed for the shooter nearest him. Soon, the two were engaged in hand-to-hand combat. It took all his strength to overpower the man and choke him until he lost consciousness.

Axel grabbed the perp's weapon and fired on the two men approaching. Both went down. Summer's pretty face was all he saw as he fought with everything inside himself to win the battle that was stacked against him from the beginning.

Someone snatched at his arms, imprisoning them behind his back. Another man wrestled the weapon from Axel's hand.

A man he didn't know stopped inches from his face. Axel had no doubt this was Ray. There was something familiar about the man who had caused so much pain.

"Where is she?" The brutality on the man's face spoke of someone who would do anything to get what they wanted.

Axel's stomach clenched when he thought of what this man would do to Summer. "There's no one here but me."

What passed for a smile didn't touch Ray's eyes or wipe the cruelty from his face. "You're protecting her. You know what kind of person she is and you're willing to give your life for her?" The amazement in Ray's voice was clear.

When Axel didn't respond, the trafficker turned to one of his people. "Search the place. She's here."

Ray's attention never left Axel as the armed men began sweeping each room. It didn't take them long to find Summer. She was brought out alone. Where was Brayden?

Axel couldn't take his eyes off her. He tried to break free of his restrainer's hold but couldn't. The terror on her face as she was forced over to where Ray stood made him angry with himself. He'd let her down. He'd promised to protect her, and he'd let her down.

Ray strode over to her and grabbed a handful of her hair.

Summer cried out in pain and shrank as far away as she could get. "Please, no, Ray. The baby. Think about the baby."

A smirk crossed his face as Ray yanked her closer. "I don't want the money I'd get for it as much as I need to eliminate the problem you represent."

"Stop it," Axel yelled. Ray jerked his head back to Axel before motioning to one of his people, who slugged Axel's stomach. The breath flew from his body. The man restraining him was all that held him up.

"You've caused me a lot of problems, Summer," Ray ground out. "This is all your fault. Now I'm going to have to kill him. Are you proud of yourself?" Ray released her and shoved her away.

"Please, Ray, don't," she pleaded. "You don't have to kill him. He's not part of this. It's me you want. Let him be." There were tears falling down her face as she begged for Axel's life.

Ray simply laughed. "Get them both outside." The man restraining Axel forced him from the house. Two men flanked him, all heavily armed. Summer was pulled along by her captor.

Not like this. Axel couldn't let it end like this. He couldn't lose her. He…loved her. *Please, God. We need You.*

One thing was clear: Summer had made Axel want to join the world of the living again. He wanted to become a better person. After Erin's death, he never believed love would be possible for him again. Never thought he had anything else to give another woman. But when he looked at Summer, he saw a future with her, and he wanted to have the chance to see if she felt the same way about him. He understood that she'd need time to heal before she could fully love and trust any man again. He'd wait for her as long as she needed because she was worth it.

Summer's frantic gaze locked with his. She silently pleaded with him to do something. Once more, he fought to free himself from their enemies but couldn't. All he had was his words to assure her. "It's going to be okay, Summer." But would it? Would they find a way to escape Ray or die together here in this frozen world.

"Isn't that sweet." Ray came over to stand in front of Axel. "What are you going to do? Fight all of us to save her?" He jerked his head back toward Summer. "You know what she is. She's not worth it."

Anger boiled up inside Axel. "She's worth everything. Everything you took from her."

Ray smirked and motioned to one of his men who put a gun to Axel's head. Ray would make Summer watch him die.

"You want him to live?" Ray asked Summer. "Then you'll tell me where you hid the thumb drive." Her surprise confirmed what Ray had accused her of. "Yes, I know what you did. I kept track of the blank thumb drives in the office. It took me a while to realize one was missing, but when I did, I knew it was you." Ray's eyes gleamed with some dark pleasure at seeing her in pain. "What's it going to be, Summer?"

She shook her head. "I'll never tell you where I hid it and I made sure to get word to the police. They'll have it soon enough."

Just a tiny amount of doubt showed on Ray's face. "You're lying. There's no way you had time to do such a thing."

Summer lifted her chin. "Are you willing to risk everything and anger your boss, Vitaliy? She wasn't happy with you before. I can't imagine what she'll say when she learns how badly you messed up this time."

Ray strode angrily over to her and slapped her hard. Summer's head flew sideways. Axel fought against his restraints but couldn't break their hold.

"You're lying." Ray kept his hand raised and inches from her face. Summer never flinched away. It broke Axel to imagine the things she'd gone through at this man's hands that were far greater than a slap to the face.

Something caught Axel's attention near the front of the house. In the open doorway, Brayden leaned against the frame.

No. Stay hidden, he mouthed, trying to warn his friend.

Brayden didn't listen. He stumbled from the doorway. Axel expected him to be shot immediately. He looked a lot like Brayden.

"What are you doing here?" Ray dropped his hand and crossed the snowy landscape to the porch where Brayden was now barely hanging on. Ray saw the amount of blood Brayden had lost. "What happened?"

"Jimmy, I figured you were behind this somehow!" Brayden exclaimed. "I recognized some of your old friends from back in the day shooting at me. I knew you had to be up to something bad on the mountain near my place, but I still can't believe you'd do something this awful."

Jimmy. Axel recognized the name immediately because Brayden had spoken of the cousin who was like a brother to him. The one his family had taken in when Jimmy was just a child. Jimmy—Ray was Brayden's family.

TWELVE

Brayden was related to Ray? Summer saw the resemblance between the two now. She'd heard Ray talk about his strait-laced brother who tried to get him to change, but she'd never put it together that Brayden was that brother. Ray's people had shot his own brother.

"I knew you were up to something bad," Brayden rasped while gripping the porch rail, his weak body swaying.

Ray appeared contrite for half a second.

"Dad was right about you," Brayden muttered with disgust on his face. "There's something terribly wrong inside you, Jimmy. Mom was just too blind to see until you killed her and Dad."

Summer was mesmerized by the exchange between the two cousinss. Something dreadful had happened to this family. Was it what had caused Ray to become this monster?

"They got what they deserved!" Ray yelled angrily before regaining his composure. "Look, I'm sorry you got yourself involved in this, Brayden. You were always good to me, but I guess I knew having a deputy for a 'brother' was going to get in my way." Ray smirked at his cousin before he started for Summer. "We need to get this over with and clear out in case someone around called the cops." He glanced over his shoulder. "Like my brother."

"You don't have to do this, Ray." Summer clutched her belly as a sharp pain had her doubling over. Her baby. She couldn't let him kill her baby. She pulled in several breaths before saying, "Just leave. We won't tell anyone."

Ray stepped inches away from her. "You think I don't know as soon as I'm gone that you and your friends here will give the evidence you stole from me to the cops." He grabbed her arm painfully. "I destroyed everything else. All the computers, everything that ties me to… Where'd you put it."

She lifted her face to his and stared him down. Ray grabbed her arm so tight, his fingers dug into it. "Where is it?"

"Leave her alone. She doesn't have your stuff," Axel yelled, drawing Ray's attention to him.

"You care for her." Ray seemed surprised. His attention returned to Summer. "And you have feelings for him. This is the last chance to tell the truth before he dies."

"No. Please, Ray, no," Summer pleaded.

Ray's glee was clear in the smile that spread across his face.

The man holding the gun on Axel suddenly jerked toward his right. Summer caught a glimpse of an injured Camo flying toward Ray. Camo grabbed hold of Ray's leg. Ray screamed as the dog's canines buried deep.

"Get him off me!" Ray raged while slapping at the dog.

Axel grabbed for the distracted man's weapon, and Summer ran to help him as the man fought to keep possession of the gun.

"Get down, Summer!" Axel yelled, finally gaining full control of the handgun. He aimed the weapon on the man, who raised his hands in surrender.

Summer hit the frozen ground and covered her head as

Ray's men fired on Axel, who returned shots. He scooped Summer up and ducked behind the truck.

"Stay here," he instructed. "I'm going to get Brayden."

Summer peeked through the window of the truck in time to see Ray finally managed to shove the injured dog off him and whirl toward Axel ready to shoot. Before he could fire a single shot, the woods around them lit up with headlights.

Dozens of vehicles moved in led by a snowplow. The driver of the plow let the rest of the vehicles pass by. As they drew close, the sheriff's department emblem was emblazoned on the side of several. An ambulance was there as well. Joy rose in her chest. They were saved. Axel's call had gone through after all. She hadn't been sure. More than half an hour had passed since he'd placed the call and she'd begun to lose hope.

Axel grabbed the fading Brayden and hauled him over to the truck.

Soon, the sheriff's department was engaged in battle with the attackers. Axel edged toward the back of the truck and assisted.

Summer caught movement to her left and whirled toward it. Ray loomed beside her. He grabbed her arm and hauled her up beside him with the gun to her head. "You're coming with me. I want that thumb drive." He yanked her along with him to the closest vehicle.

She tried to scream but Ray clamped his hand over her mouth. "Oh, no you don't. You're going to show me where you hid that evidence."

Her frantic eyes searched for Axel. In the chaos around them, would he notice she was in danger?

Ray reached the vehicle and opened the door. He shoved her inside. Before he could get in after her, Axel materialized beside him and shoved his weapon against Ray's temple.

"It's over, Ray. Give up."

Ray tried to get the handgun into position to shoot Summer, but Axel pressed his weapon harder against the man's temple. "I wouldn't do that if I were you."

Throwing daggers Summer's way, Ray eventually dropped the weapon and raised his hands. Axel grabbed the gun and tucked it in his pocket. "Are you hurt?" he asked her.

Summer shook her head. "No, I'm okay." She leaned back against the seat, her hands shaking at how close to death she'd come once more. She noticed that Ray's uninjured men were now surrendering.

Ray saw that he was defeated and yet he wasn't going quietly. He continued to rage at Summer and assure her he'd make her pay for betraying him.

A sheriff's deputy came over. "I've got him." He took control of Ray. After searching him and finding yet another weapon, the deputy handcuffed him and led him away.

"Let's get you out of here." Axel held out his hand. Summer clasped it and let him help her from the vehicle. She wrapped her arms around his waist and held him close.

"Is it really over?" she asked, her voice shaking. After so long, was she finally free of Ray?

"It is," he said softly against her ear. "It really is."

"Brayden." She remembered how seriously injured he was. "He needs help."

Axel clasped her hand and together they hurried over to where Brayden was receiving medical assistance.

"How is he?" Axel asked the EMT examining his friend's wound.

"He's lost a lot of blood," the paramedic replied. "We need to get him to the hospital right away."

Axel nodded and stepped back as Brayden was taken to one of the waiting ambulances.

Another EMT came over to Summer. "Ma'am, you should let me examine you. You've obviously been through quite an ordeal. How far along are you? Are you experiencing any pain?"

"Yes, some earlier, but I'm okay right now." Summer couldn't imagine how awful she looked. "I think I'm around eight months."

The EMT gave her a curious look and she did her best to explain what she was certain of.

"I promise I'm going to take good care of you," the paramedic assured her. She held on to Axel's hand while the EMT did the examination. "You're in remarkably good health all things considered. Still, we need to get you to the hospital to run some further tests."

"He's right, Summer," Axel told her.

"I'm not leaving without you." And she wouldn't. Then Summer noticed something disturbing. "Camo." The dog heard his name and limped over. At first, Summer thought it was the injury he'd sustained with the snowcat accident until she saw blood above the old injury.

"I'm so sorry, boy." Axel knelt beside his injured friend.

"Here, let me take a look." A second EMT brought his bag over and carefully treated Camo's leg while Axel told him about the previous injury. "Looks like the bullet went straight through. I don't see any serious damage from the earlier accident. I'll bandage it up, but I would suggest you take him to your vet as soon as possible."

"I will, thank you," Axel assured him.

Sheriff Wyatt McCallister and two of his deputies came over and introduced themselves.

"Are you the one who called this in?" he asked Axel.

Axel told him yes. "I wasn't sure if your dispatcher got enough from the call to pinpoint our location."

Ray and the rest of his people were being cuffed and loaded into the waiting cruisers.

"Thank you for saving my deputy." The sheriff shook his head. "This will take a lot of sorting out." His attention went to Summer. "How do you fit into all of this, ma'am?"

Axel clasped her hand as she told him her story. Summer didn't realize that she was crying as she spoke until she'd finished.

"I'm so sorry that happened to you, Summer," the sheriff said gently.

Summer felt the weight of the past years lift from her shoulders. "He said he has law enforcement working for him." She waited for the sheriff to deny it. A hard look came and went.

"Unfortunately, it's possible." He explained about what happened previously when an officer and the district attorney had been arrested for assisting a human trafficking ring. "We'll need to get both of your statements soon."

Now that Ray was in custody, Summer was more than happy to assist. "The thumb drive—I almost forgot about it." She explained about stashing it in a secure place at the house where she and Ray and the other members of his crew stayed. "There are other victims being held there, or at least there were, unless Ray moved them. Oh, and there was a woman who visited once. She appeared to be in charge. Her name was Vitaliy."

Sheriff McCallister had listened intently. "Sounds like we'll need to get the feds involved since this appears to be an international ring. We couldn't link the previous arrests to anything international. With the drive and your witness testimony, we can make arrests that will bring down this ring and hopefully get those young women home."

"There's something else." Summer hesitated. What if

Ray had just been bragging…or what if it were all true. "Ray claimed he killed some people years ago."

Axel remembered what Brayden had said. "I think Brayden can shed some light on what happened." He told them about Brayden calling Ray by the name of his brother, Jimmy. "Actually, I remember Brayden saying once that Jimmy was his cousin and not his brother. His family took Jimmy in when he had no one else. It sounds like Jimmy killed his own parents as well as Brayden's." Axel's mouth thinned. "That's one disturbed person."

"We'll get Brayden's take on everything as soon as he's cleared by the doctor." The sheriff then focused on Summer. "I'd feel better if you'd go to the hospital to be checked out. After what you've both gone through and considering your lack of medical care, it would be a good idea to get checked out"

Axel turned to her. "He's right. You need to make sure the baby is fine."

"I'd be happy to take you. Give me a few minutes." The sheriff stepped away to speak with his people.

"I can't believe this happened." Summer still couldn't let go of the fear Ray had instilled in her. How long would it take before she felt safe?

Axel pushed hair from her eyes "It's over, Summer."

As she looked into his handsome face, a sharp pain in her lower abdomen had her clutching her stomach.

"What's wrong?" Axel's worried expression swam before her.

"I think the baby is coming." She doubled over.

"We've got to get you to the hospital. Now." Axel waved the sheriff over. "She's in labor."

"Let's go," McCallister said.

Axel helped her to the sheriff's cruiser and then got in beside her while Sheriff McCallister hit the lights.

Tears swam in her eyes. She was finally going to meet her child and she had nothing to offer—not even a home.

"We'll figure it all out…together," Axel whispered. "You're not alone. You'll never be alone again."

As she looked at the man who had risked everything for her, she saw the future she so desperately prayed for could be hers.

"You did good, Mamma," Axel told her when the precious baby girl was placed in her arms. The smile she gave was filled with exhaustion and he couldn't remember anything ever looking so beautiful before.

After everything they'd gone through, to have a new life come from such darkness seemed the perfect conclusion to Ray's reign of terror.

Ten little toes. Ten perfect fingers. A small version of her mother with fine blond hair. The wonder of life made everything they'd gone through to get to this point seem trivial.

"You're sure she's healthy?" Summer asked the nurse again.

"She's perfect," the nurse said with a smile.

Axel sat down beside her and watched the baby in her arms. "Have you thought of a name for her yet?"

Summer didn't hesitate. "I want to name her after my mother. Her name is Abigail." She watched in awe as her daughter looked up at her. "Actually, my mother's name is Abigail Elizabeth. I'm named after her, too."

"Abigail Elizabeth is a pretty name. Your daughter will be named after you and your mother." Axel touched the baby's hand and his heart melted when she latched on to his finger. "Abigail Elizabeth needs to know what a strong woman her mother is. She will be proud of you for what you've overcome."

Summer seemed to fight back tears. "I can finally be Elizabeth again. Summer is dead to me. I told myself that until I truly became free of Ray, I couldn't be the person I was before. Now I can. I'm Elizabeth."

Axel smiled, realizing again that he loved her with all his heart. "Yes, you are."

As she looked into his eyes something shifted in hers. "I'd be dead if it weren't for you, Axel. I owe you everything."

He reached up and brushed away the tears. "You changed my life. If I hadn't met you, I have no doubt I'd still be living in isolation clinging to my grief. I don't want to be that man anymore. You've made me want to be better. You've made..." He hesitated, unable to lay his heart on the line yet. She'd need time to rebuild her life with her child. "You've made me believe in love again, *Elizabeth*, when I thought I'd lost it. I care for you, and I want to be there for you in whatever way that looks like. As a friend and a neighbor, however you want me to be part of your life."

"You gave me hope, too, Axel. I'd forgotten what that felt like." A sob escaped her. "And I care about you, too, but..."

"You need time to heal," he finished for her.

"Yes." Her eyes pleaded with him to understand.

For Axel it was easy. "I'll give you all the time you need. You survived so much. You're a strong woman. You will get through this. What happened won't define you. It will grow you."

With her tears falling he carefully gathered her close and held her while she cried.

When he'd spotted her on that road the day before, Axel couldn't have predicted the journey the two of them would take together. Or the results of that journey, which would prove to be life-altering for both. Thanks to God, everything had worked out. Brayden was going to be okay. He was here at the same hospital as Elizabeth and the baby so Axel could check on his friend, and the sheriff had volunteered to keep Camo until Axel was ready to come home. He felt at peace with the world for the first time in years.

As difficult as it had been, he was grateful for the struggle he and Elizabeth had gone through because he'd met this amazing woman whom he couldn't wait to get to know better.

EPILOGUE

One year later...

The familiar countryside near her former Amish home brought fresh tears to her eyes. Elizabeth glanced back at the sleeping baby.

More than a year had passed since she and Axel had been rescued. It made her proud that because of her, dozens of women had been recovered.

And Elizabeth was proud of the progress she'd made through the past year. She'd gotten professional help after what she'd endured and had slowly started to recover from Ray's trauma and rebuild her life with her child.

Watching Abby grow had been a big part of her healing. She'd learned to stand on her own two feet and discovered she was stronger than she imagined.

With the help of Axel, Abram and Lainey, and her therapist, she no longer blamed herself for what Ray did.

And she and Axel had grown closer. She'd learned what true love really looked like. She'd known she cared for Axel but over this past year, she'd let go of her doubts and accepted that she did deserve to be loved. Axel had shown her how a real man loved, and it was nothing like the hurt Ray put her through. It was gentle and patient. Just like Axel.

She'd slowly grown more confident and reached out to her parents through letters. They were amazingly supportive and anxious to see her.

Now she was ready. Sheriff McCallister had assured her there would be more arrests across the country and internationally thanks to the information on the thumb drive.

Vitaliy proved to be Vitaliy Babanin. A Russian aristocrat who had been on Interpol's radar for some time. Elizabeth had been heavily protected until it was time for her to testify. With her help, they'd busted up an international trafficking ring.

Two police officers from the Polson force in the next county had been taken into custody. Both appeared eager to talk to save themselves a lengthy prison sentence.

Brayden had also mended over time. Axel had been staying with him to allow Elizabeth and Abby to have his cabin.

Thanks to Brayden, the missing pieces of Jimmy's life were finally known. It was terrifying for Elizabeth to realize the house in the woods where she and the others had stayed was once Jimmy's family home which was over in the next county. At Elizabeth's suggestion, the sheriff had dug up the floor beneath the barn and found Jimmy's dad, who was believed to have left Jimmy behind. He'd never left his property but had been buried beside his wife and younger son whom Jimmy had also killed. Brayden was convinced Jimmy had something to do with his own parents' deaths as well.

The file marked Barn that the sheriff recovered from the thumb drive contained detailed journal entries and photos of the murder of Jimmy's family. The sheriff believed Jimmy kept them as some type of trophy. He was much more disturbed than Elizabeth had even realized.

"Is this it?" Axel asked, drawing her attention away from Ray's deadly past.

She spotted the mailbox next to the drive that led to her parents' home. Everything still looked the same and yet nine years had passed.

Elizabeth had told her parents everything that happened to her. Her mamm wrote back and told her how heartbroken they all were for what she'd suffered. They were excited to meet their granddaughter one day.

After months of exchanging letters, it was finally time to see her family face-to-face.

"This is it." The nervous butterflies returned. How could she face them after everything that happened?

Axel reached for her hand. "They love you. They're excited to see you again, Elizabeth. Remember, they thought they'd lost you forever."

She smiled over at him. Elizabeth wouldn't have gotten through all of this without him. She loved him so much and couldn't wait to marry him one day, but she had to see her parents and brothers first. Had to know they still loved her.

Axel had assured her he'd give her whatever she needed, even if it meant having to say goodbye to her. The thought of losing him hurt physically.

After the terrible things Ray had put her through, Elizabeth never expected to feel anything again, especially not love.

"You know if you want to stay with your family for a while…"

She didn't let him finish, but she loved him for his selflessness. "I love my family and I loved being Amish, but I can't go back to that life again. It isn't who I am anymore. You and Abby are my future." She prayed the future would include visits with her family, though.

"I love you," he murmured. Every time he said the endearment, her heart became lighter.

"I love you, too."

Axel squeezed her hand before turning onto the driveway.

From her car seat, Abby watched the passing scenery and kicked her feet…just like she had in the womb.

The trees lining the drive were covered in snow. The path curved around the property in snakelike fashion until they reached the clearing near the house.

"Oh." The word slipped from Elizabeth's lips when she got her first glimpse of her former home. "It still looks the same." Only there were signs of aging all around from the peeling paint to the sagging porch.

Axel stopped the truck in front of the home. Elizabeth couldn't take her eyes off it. While she watched, steeped in the past, the front door opened, and her past rose from her memories to become a flesh-and-blood living being.

"*Mamm*." Her mother still looked the same—maybe a little older—but still the same. And *Daed* was still a good foot taller than his wife. But the biggest change was found in the two young boys she'd left behind. They were no longer boys but young men. At nineteen, Peter would be finished with his *rumspringa*. Eli would be starting his.

Following a bit slower, the family dog, Pepper, came out onto the porch, her dark fur showing white around her face.

Camo had come with them on the trip. When he spotted Pepper, he grew excited.

"Settle down, boy," Axel told the dog.

Tears filled Elizabeth's eyes and she rushed from the vehicle and started for the porch. Behind her, Axel climbed out and got Abby from her car seat. He followed along with Camo, who went up the steps to sniff Pepper.

Elizabeth stopped once she reached the porch and suddenly all the old doubts and fears resurfaced. She'd left them. How could they ever find it in their hearts to forgive her foolishness.

But one look at her *mamm*'s face confirmed she'd been worried for nothing. *Mamm* closed the space between them and gathered Elizabeth into her arms, weeping and laughing at the same time.

"You're home. My little girl is home."

Daed and the boys got in on the hugs and all Elizabeth's concerns faded away. She was loved. By these precious people. By her baby. And by the man who had taught her what true love really looked like.

* * * * *

Dear Reader,

I hope you enjoyed Summer and Axel's story about finding redemption. *Ambush in the Mountains* focuses on the dark world of human trafficking, and one person's struggle to escape and to save others caught up in this devastating crime against the innocent. This fight is dear to my heart. I pray that God will break the bonds of those struggling both physically and emotionally and set them free, that there will be an end to human trafficking, and that all those who live in darkness and fear will be brought into His light.

For Summer, protecting her baby gives her the courage to escape her captor, yet without the help of Axel, a wounded warrior dealing with issues himself, she might not have survived the trafficker determined to silence her before the truth can be made known.

But thanks be to God, and to some brave people both Amish and *Englischer* along the way, Summer finds true freedom after so many years of being held captive. And together, with Axel's help, the two find their way into the light and to a future filled with the happiness they both so richly deserve.

Mary Alford